Running from a scandal that ruined his life, Isaac Twain accepts a teaching position at Hambden University where, three months prior, Professor John Conlon stopped a campus nightmare by stepping in front of an active shooter.

When John and Isaac become faculty advisors for the school's literary magazine, their professional relationship evolves. Despite the strict code of conduct forbidding faculty fraternization, they delve into a secret affair—until Simon arrives.

Isaac's violent ex threatens not only their careers, but also John's life. His PTSD triggered, John must come to terms with that bloody day on College Green while Isaac must accept the heartbreak his secrets have wrought.

WE STILL LIVE

Sara Dobie Bauer

A NineStar Press Publication

Published by NineStar Press
P.O. Box 91792,
Albuquerque, New Mexico, 87199 USA.
www.ninestarpress.com

We Still Live

Printed in the USA
First Edition
December, 2019

Print ISBN: 978-1-951057-80-0

Also available in eBook, ISBN: 978-1-951057-79-4

Warning: This book contains sexually explicit content, which may only be suitable for mature readers, scenes of graphic violence/gore, school shooting, past trauma, PTSD/post-traumatic stress, depression, anxiety, attempted suicide, and mentions of past infidelity.

To those who suffer and seek healing.

Chapter One

DR. ISAAC TWAIN stood in a cozy house surrounded by strangers, where a forced jubilation floated like stale smoke. The house was something out of the Shire, a hobbit home for humans, on a hilltop in Lothos, Ohio, overlooking Hambden University's campus.

Isaac had been dragged around the party earlier and introduced. The head of the English Department called him an "emergency hire." Emergency because two of their professors had resigned a week before the semester started when they realized they couldn't come back, not after what happened.

The unfamiliar faces of his new coworkers floated in and out of Isaac's attention. In the overwarm, crowded kitchen, two older ladies smiled up at him and tried asking about his work, his life—did he have a wife?—but he ducked their questions like a soldier ducks bullets. For a time, he hovered among them with his glass of wine until a delightfully disorganized bookshelf in a room off the main foyer caught his eye, and he took solace.

Stepping inside, he cast a glance over what had to be someone's office. An antique oak desk anchored the space, though its surface was bare and dusty from nonuse. A couple of framed band posters decorated the walls, but the only name Isaac recognized was Freddie Mercury. Trying not to snoop, he turned his attention back to the initial object of interest.

Books of all shapes and sizes crammed into the shelves at odd angles. Half were alphabetized, as if their owner had once considered organization and admitted defeat. In the top right corner sat a bobblehead, some kind of rodent with a red W on its chest. Isaac bopped the critter on the head, and it nodded in response.

An author named John Conlon dominated an entire half shelf. Isaac grabbed a book with bright binding—young adult, if the cover was anything to go by. He set his glass of wine on the nearby table, empty but for a photograph of a smiling couple with dark hair (whoever lived here was apparently not a fan of clutter) and flipped pages. He read the first line—*It wasn't meant to happen that summer, but by then, Declan understood the things he meant and the things he did were often at odds*—until a stranger arrived at his side.

"Hey, newbie. You hiding?"

Isaac looked up to find an overgrown frat boy with spiked blond hair and a square-shaped head staring back at him. "Maybe," Isaac said. He lifted his chin toward the kitchen. "It's claustrophobic in there."

The man shrugged. "What can I say? We're overbearing, given the right amount of alcohol." He extended his hand. "I'm Tommy Dewars."

Isaac slid the Conlon book back where it belonged and accepted Tommy's greeting. "Isaac Twain."

"We're playing the name game later. See if you remember everybody. If you mess up, you're fired."

"Yeah, sure."

He squinted up at Isaac. "Not to be weird, but English professors aren't usually seven feet of solid muscle."

Isaac almost choked on his drink. Granted, people often commented on his height and physique, but

Tommy's remark still caught him off guard. "I used to run marathons," he said. "But I'm a geek on the inside. Promise." When Tommy smiled, Isaac tipped his head toward the dusty desk. "This your place?"

"Mine? No, God, no. I live in a shithole closer to campus. This is John's place. He's driving back from Wisconsin today, but he should be here soon. How long have you been in town? Heard you moved up from North Carolina?"

"South Carolina. Charleston." He finished half the glass of wine in one go. "I've only been here a couple days."

Tommy's wrinkled plaid button-down untucked from his jeans when he scratched his belly, and he sipped what appeared to be whiskey. "Why the hell would you move to Ohio from Charleston?"

Isaac shrugged as the boisterous kitchen conversation spilled down the hall. "Change of scenery."

Somewhere, a glass dropped and shattered. Disinterested, Isaac paid the disturbance no mind so was ill prepared for a sudden assault. He huffed out a breath when Tommy suddenly tackled him to the floor, both their glasses flying. Isaac held his hands up, bracing for a punch...until he realized he wasn't being attacked.

Tommy, eyes wide, scrambled off Isaac and sat back on his heels. "Shit, I am so sorry."

Isaac leaned up on his elbows. "You okay?"

Jaw clenched, Tommy sputtered a chuckle. "Apparently not." He stood and helped Isaac to his feet. He laughed some more and brushed at the front of Isaac's blazer. "I, uh..." He pressed his lips together and glanced behind him. "New habits, I guess. Jesus." He smacked Isaac on the shoulder. "Seriously, are you okay?"

Isaac's heart thudded in his chest, but he still said, "Fine."

"I need to get you another drink."

Isaac picked up their dropped glasses, spilled but not broken. "It's all right."

"You came at a really bad time, man."

"I know." He did know. Well, he knew enough. School shootings were practically a weekly occurrence. Six people had died in a campus shooting at Hambden the spring before, although that was his only detail. Details seemed too heavy, the number of lives lost countrywide like rocks tied to the necks of those drowning in despair.

"What are you teaching this semester?"

"Mostly composition," Isaac said, silently agreeing to Tommy's need to just move on and forget about the impromptu tackle. "Guess they want to make sure I know what I'm talking about before they give me upperclassmen."

Tommy frowned at the empty glasses Isaac placed on a shelf. "Composition. You don't even get English majors in there. You'll probably be dealing with a bunch of business nerds trying to learn how to write office memos."

"Thrilling."

Close as they were to the foyer, Isaac was the first to notice the front door opening. A student walked inside. The kid dragged a heavy-looking suitcase behind him. Dressed as he was in a slim-fitting button-down, Isaac immediately assumed preppy, although that assumption altered and changed when taking into account the tight black jeans, Converse sneakers, and shaggy hair the color of caramel and chocolate—a mass of waves and curls that fell down the back of his neck but not quite to his shoulders.

The kid pushed his hair out of the way and looked up, eyes finding Isaac and flashing a moment of panicked nonrecognition before seeing Tommy.

"Um." Isaac pointed toward the new arrival.

Tommy turned and shouted, "John! My man!"

Not a student, then.

Tommy wrapped John in a hug that actually lifted his feet off the ground. Isaac imagined it wouldn't be difficult. The new guy might have been average height, but he was gangly, skin and bones.

Tommy ruffled his hair. "Have you lost weight?"

John grumbled and scratched his face with his middle finger. "What are you freeloaders doing in my house?" His voice was surprisingly resonant for someone Isaac considered "pretty." At John's pronouncement, crows of approval rang from every direction.

"Come meet Isaac," Tommy said.

John wiped his palms on his jeans before reaching out to shake, and Isaac's large hand dwarfed his.

"Isaac Twain is the newest addition to our special corner of Hambden hell. Isaac, this is John Conlon."

John brushed more hair out of his face. "Nice to—"

"John *Conlon*?"

John and Tommy froze.

Isaac jerked his thumb over his shoulder. "The books on the shelf. Those are yours?"

John's face, immobile in what looked like dread a moment before, melted into relief, tinged with a bit of blush. "Oh, yeah. You've read?"

"No, but I should. You've published a lot of books. You must be good."

John's nose wrinkled, and he looked away.

Tommy shook him by the shoulders. "John is an amazing writer. He had a story published in *The New Yorker* when he was, like, five. Are you working on anything right now?"

John glanced at the bookshelf. "Not lately."

"You need a drink," Tommy said.

John's eyes widened on a big breath. "God, yes, I do."

"Nice to meet you," Isaac said, but John just nodded quickly, smile thin, before allowing himself to be herded farther into the house toward the sound of quiet laughter and clinking bottles.

Isaac felt it then—an outsider's emptiness. He became a nervous-looking coat rack in the corner, a terrified tree waiting for the ax. As the party doubled in auditory volume, he bemoaned his spilled wine. Was it okay for him to leave? It wasn't like he was supposed to make a speech. He was only there because he figured it was the easiest way to meet everyone before the first official faculty meeting, but he'd been standing around too long. He wanted to run.

Out of curiosity, he reopened John's book from earlier and read the front flap. It was a coming-of-age story about a gay kid in the Midwest. He flipped to the back, and a picture of John stared back at him. He'd assumed the guy was tired when they first met, but no; apparently, John had perpetual bedroom eyes, and his hair was always an artful mess. He skimmed...*creative writing professor at Hambden University...gay rights activist...Converse-wearer and "old-people music" enthusiast.*

All arrows pointed to John's probable sexual preference for men. A spark of interest flickered but quickly went out. True, John Conlon was what most people would consider beautiful, but he wasn't Isaac's type. John was the kind of man butch guys fought over in gay clubs, but he was too small for Isaac, too fragile-looking, girly. After all he'd been through, the last thing Isaac wanted was someone feminine.

A thin figure ducked into the library and literally hid against the doorframe. He took a long drink of something brown and leaned his head back. "It's not good when you want to hide in your own house."

"Library is the best place for it," Isaac said.

John kicked away from the wall. "Tommy mentioned you just moved here? I've been in Lothos forever, so if you need anything…" He examined Isaac from his brown boat shoes to the top of his blond head. John's large eyes, dark green, seemed bottomless—drowning pools of intellect and soul—only slightly overshadowed by his thick eyebrows.

Isaac took a step backward in response to his inspection. "Um, Tommy mentioned you were on your way back from Wisconsin?"

"I grew up there. My family's still there. I took the summer… I…um…" He closed his eyes and squeezed the bridge of his nose. "I'm usually really good at finishing sentences."

A bubble of amusement rose in Isaac's chest.

"You look like I feel."

"And how do you feel?" Isaac asked.

"Like I want to bury my head in a hole. Or get messy drunk." He lifted his glass in an unreciprocated toast and drank.

"This is going to sound really insensitive, but can I ask you a question?"

John shrugged.

"The shooting."

John coughed once, quickly. A loud laugh from the hallway made him startle and look over his shoulder.

Isaac could have backpedaled—*should* have, based on the way his coworker now resembled a spooked deer—but in for a penny. "Do you mind me asking what happened?"

John stared at him for a long moment before his mouth curved into something like a smile. The intelligent scrutiny of his gaze disappeared in a haze of what Isaac assumed was memory. Then he said, "You don't know," with an abundance of relief.

"I know it's very ignorant of me, and possibly callous, but no."

John traced his pale finger along the edge of the bookcase. "It was on College Green last June. The College of Arts and Sciences award ceremony. One of our students started shooting, and he eventually shot himself."

"You were there?"

John laughed, which seemed sorely out of place. "Yeah, I was there. All of us were there." He leaned closer, so close Isaac smelled bourbon on his breath. "A word of advice: don't ask anyone else about it unless you're really good with tears."

Isaac shifted from one foot to the other. "You're not crying."

"No." He finished his glass and spun around. "I need more alcohol." It felt like a brush-off, an escape.

"John. I didn't mean to upset you."

"You didn't." He tapped his palm on the doorframe and looked back. "You know, you don't have to stay here hiding. It's painful watching introverts try to acclimate in social situations."

Isaac smirked. "How do you know I'm an introvert?"

"We recognize our own kind, man. Every day of my life, my mantra is 'Don't be awkward.'"

"How's that working for you?"

"Not well." John smiled, rows of white teeth on display, and Isaac felt like the sun shined on his face. "Nice meeting you, Isaac. Now, go the fuck home."

Relieved, Isaac dug his leather coat from the hall closet. Isaac having come from the South, the Midwestern nights chilled his bones. He did his best not to draw attention as he snuck to the front door and out into evening. He glanced back once and pondered John Conlon, a contradiction of a man. Not a student but a teacher; not a yuppie but a man who used "fuck" at faculty parties. Not a friend yet, but maybe.

Chapter Two

THE WHOLE THIRD floor smelled like antiseptic—scrubbed clean as though the shooting had happened there, in Ellis Hall, even though it hadn't. Isaac could see the tragic site from his office, though, its green grass lush in late summer. He even walked by a huge altar that morning, in remembrance of those lost, and paused to look at a couple pictures. They were meaningless to him—smiling faces sad in their absence. His empathy stretched to a general idea but nothing specific, although he knew the same could not be said for his coworkers. In Ellis Hall, he felt their pain like air-conditioning in winter.

A splotchy, white-and-gray sycamore practically poked through his window as he looked over lesson plans and pretended to focus, even as his cell phone vibrated in the desk. Again. After the fourth alert, he'd shoved it in a drawer as though putting it away would make it disappear, make the caller disappear. Like the town of Lothos, Isaac Twain had his own tragedies.

Cleo—the self-proclaimed English Department "administrative diva"—walked in. Her floral perfume prefaced her arrival when she floated gracefully through his open door. "Excuse me, Dr. Twain?"

"I said you could call me Isaac, Cleo."

When she didn't respond, he looked up to find her chewing on her red, painted bottom lip. She had on a baby-doll dress, oddly adorned with skulls, and six-inch stiletto heels. She was an attractive amalgam of fifties housewife and Halloween.

"Do you want to call me doctor?" he asked.

"It makes me feel important," she said.

Cleo seemed perky and kind, so he smiled and gave her that one. "What do you need?"

Isaac had met Cleo earlier in the week for coffee, to get to know her, as she was his guide until the students arrived and classes began. With bright-red hair and blue eyes, she smelled of roses and did most of the talking.

Her heels made no sound on the gray-blue carpet when she came closer. "Just one more signature on your employment paperwork. The awkward one."

"The awkward one?"

"The departmental nonfraternization policy. It's very fire and brimstone." She shrugged and held a paper between them. "Not that there's a lot of hot chicks running around the English Department."

No way was he touching that one. He cleared his throat and signed quickly before handing it back.

"How are you settling in? You found an apartment, right, on Union Street? Great location." She played with her hands, crumpling the corner of his contract. "I mean, if you drink. Do you drink?"

"I, um—"

"You probably drink grown-up drinks, don't you, like Tommy and John?" She took a deep breath. "They swear by the hard stuff, but I need to do mixed drinks, you know? I like tonic. I'm seriously not annoying. I'm just nervous."

He glanced around his office. "About me?"

"No." She tilted her head, and her red curls tumbled to one side. "You seem cool. And you're older, so you obviously have plenty of teaching experience—not to say you're old. I'm sorry. See? I'm a mess." She threw her hands in the air and almost dropped his paperwork.

Isaac tried very hard not to laugh. "Cleo. Sit down, please."

She sat in the leather chair across from his desk.

"Why are you nervous?"

"You can't feel it?"

He shook his head.

"The whole campus feels heavier. Quieter. Like it's just waiting for something else to go wrong." She glanced up at him, forehead creased in the middle. "I know you weren't here last year when it happened, but students get here in four days. They haven't been here since..." She tugged on her earlobe. "I just want this year to be okay."

"It will be." It was what she needed to hear. As a man who'd spent the last decade lying, Isaac knew how to read other people. He sat up straight in his chair because his advice mixed with his overall bearing usually made people listen. "I'm serious, Cleo."

"I know." She smiled. "Thanks, Dr. Twain."

He stood when she stood. "Hey, I meant to ask you a favor."

"Anything!"

"You update the English Department website, right?"

Her blue eyes went to the sky. "I know it's super basic and boring, but that's really all I have time to design."

"No, it's not that." He put his hands in his pockets and tried not to look as suspicious as he felt. "I was wondering if you could not add me to the website as a new faculty member? Could you leave my name off?"

She squinted. "Are you in witness protection?"

"I just don't like having an online presence."

"Oh. Sure, no biggie." She winked. "I understand the Man is watching."

"Right. Thanks, Cleo. I really appreciate it." His shoulders ached. He dropped them when he realized they hovered up near his ears.

Behind them, the hallway erupted in voices. Isaac followed Cleo to the door and saw a bunch of faculty—some from the English Department party and others Isaac had yet to meet. In the center was John with Tommy at his side, standing close like a secret service agent.

Cleo shrieked. "John!"

She rushed into his arms, almost knocking him over, and John laughed into her hair. They shared a few quiet words, but Isaac had more important things to do: namely, plan a semester. He backed into his office but not before his new boss—and new head of the English Department—Sonya Meeks appeared, all her long, brown hair pulled back in a severe bun that tugged on the sides of her eyes. She put her hand on John's shoulder and said, loud enough for everyone to hear, "Let's have a chat in my office."

Isaac closed his door and continued to ignore the phone in his desk that now vibrated with ominous frequency. It was too late to look back. If only he knew which way to move forward.

HE SKIMMED THE reading list for his slathering of composition courses when someone knocked on the door. Prepping for a new semester at a new school was going to be more work than Isaac remembered. Then again, he hadn't been the new guy in years.

"Come in."

Isaac looked up, and John leaned against the doorframe. "You look like you swallowed a frog," he said.

Isaac rubbed his forehead. "I think I forgot how to teach."

John pursed his lips together. "I relate."

"Doubtful."

He walked into the room, practically bouncing on his toes, and glanced at Isaac's as yet unhung stack of diplomas. "I'll tell you a secret. I'm a way better writer than professor."

"So why do you teach?"

"Oh, you know, shaping young minds." He rested his hands on Isaac's desk. "Let's get a drink—you, me, and Tommy. Joe's Pub. It's where all the cool teachers go."

Isaac considered his own tucked-in polo shirt, khaki pants, and boat shoes—throwbacks from living in Charleston. "I'm not cool."

"Come on."

"I can't."

"You can."

"John, I—"

Tommy shoved his head in the door. He wore glasses that day: thick, black rims that detracted from his frat-boy appearance but not enough to make him look "academic." He grinned. "So are we doing shots?"

When John smiled, his face looked even younger. Isaac bet he never needed to shave.

"Guys, I really need to work."

"You *need* to drink," Tommy said. "We'll celebrate you joining this sinking ship."

Isaac looked up. "Is it sinking?"

John plucked a book from the shelf, thumbed through it, and put it back.

When they both just stood there silently, Isaac sighed. There was no avoiding it; these guys looked willing to linger the afternoon away in his office. "Fine. First round's on me."

Tommy clapped.

The late afternoon Ohio heat felt pleasant against Isaac's throat and forearms, unlike the stifling humidity of the South. Tommy complained and wiped sweat from his brow, but John didn't say anything. When they passed the altar on College Green, he paused.

This was no altar built in June, back when the shooting had happened. It may have started then, pictures stacked, candles lit, but someone kept it in perfect order. Someone kept it free of scattered leaves, picked up candles that had fallen over, and replaced weatherworn photos of the dead with new ones.

John lurched forward and grabbed a fuzzy picture from the pile. Isaac had just enough time to see the words "Hambden hero" before John tore the picture to shreds, black-and-white paper falling like leaves on the sidewalk. No one spoke. They just kept walking, John in front, although Tommy did throw Isaac a sympathetic shrug as if to say "What can you do?"

Isaac felt like he'd missed the big twist in a horror movie, but since silence ruled, he didn't dare break it. There was a jerky anger to the way John moved now, and Isaac was in no state to be on the receiving end of a tantrum.

Lothos, Ohio, was a town of unchanging aesthetics. Tall, brick buildings covered Hambden's campus, and sprawling, green trees stretched even higher. The downtown main drag—a long strip of bars and restaurants—was Union Street, and it mimicked the university. Red bricks paved the crooked road.

They made their way past the door to Isaac's small apartment and turned left onto a street Isaac had yet to traverse. A block up, Tommy held the door to a bar, and John spun and moonwalked inside.

Isaac choked on what felt suspiciously like a giggle. "Did he just...?"

"Yeah, he does that," Tommy said. "Him and Cleo took dance lessons together a couple years back, and John realized his natural affinity for eighties breakdance." He pushed Isaac inside the bar.

Once through the door, a cloud of darkness and stale beer made Isaac's skin feel sticky. Wooden booths lined the wall to the right with pool and dartboards in the back. There was no one inside but a bartender whose face lit when he saw who'd just walked in.

"John!" he shouted—a hefty man with tattoos that crept and curled from the arms of his T-shirt.

When John reached to shake his hand, the bartender pulled him into a hug and dragged him halfway across the bar. Isaac was beginning to notice people liked picking John up, maybe because he was skinny like a rag doll. Maybe because he looked like he needed protecting.

"What's your poison today, boys?" the bartender asked.

John glanced at Isaac, already reaching for the wallet in the back of his pants. "Isaac?"

"I told you I'd get the first round."

John lifted his hands. "Your pleasure's my pleasure."

Isaac's face warmed. Those strange words coming from John should not have made him blush. "Uh, Knob Creek. Guys?"

"Nice choice, but it's a little early in the day for bourbon. IPAs for Tommy and me," John said. "Whatever you have on tap."

When Isaac went to pay, the bartender turned him down and nodded toward his coworkers. "Everything's free for our hero."

Isaac wanted to ask but didn't for fear of shattering their bit of midafternoon revelry.

They slid into a booth, Tommy and John sitting on one side and Isaac on the other. He was careful where he put his elbows since the tabletop doubled as a chalkboard, featuring pictures of penises, irate cuss words, and one phone number.

"Let's do the pissing contest," Tommy said.

"I'm sorry?"

John smiled. "Where'd you go to school?"

"Oh, uh." Isaac rattled it off like the answer to a math equation: "Vanderbilt, Auburn, and Baylor for my doctorate."

"Where's your Southern drawl?" Tommy took a gulp of beer that emptied half his glass.

"They beat it out of us when I got my teaching degree." He watched John laugh and looked away when he realized how much he liked watching John laugh. "What about you two?"

John put his hand to his chest. "Wisconsin for the Halloween party and to be close to my needy parents."

"Mama's boy."

John shrugged. "Then here for my master's."

"And I went to the illustrious Ohio State University," Tommy said.

John made a gagging sound, while Tommy puffed out his chest.

"Undergrad and master's!"

"God, you're so twisted." John finished his beer like he was trying to set a record.

"Get over yourself, you rabid badger."

John's lips curled up on one side. "Your mascot is a fucking *seed*."

Although Isaac had no idea what they talked about, the dynamic duo entertained through attitude alone.

Tommy rolled his eyes and pointed at John's beer. "Another round?"

"Yeah, get out of here, you filthy Buckeye." Once he was gone, John reached for a piece of chalk and drew the sun.

"How long have you two known each other?"

"Uhh…" John looked to be sifting through numbers in his head. "Five? Five years? That's when Tommy started working here."

"And you've been here even longer."

"It's my home."

"Not Wisconsin?"

John looked away, fingers *tap-tapping* on the chalkboard table.

Isaac knew pretty much nothing about John, so in a desperate attempt at small talk, he went for the obvious. "Tell me about your books."

John turned his head back toward Isaac, lips pressed together. A dark-brown curl hung between his eyes, but he didn't move to brush it away. "I'm a raging homo, so growing up in small-town Wisconsin wasn't the easiest."

John's word choice almost made Isaac snort bourbon. "Um."

John winced but didn't look guilty at all. "Oh, right, I'm a college professor, so I should be PC. I'm *gay.* Anyway, my family's great, but there's a lot of 'Church Ladies' up in Wisconsin. I write young adult stories that I hope help LGBTQ kids."

"I'm sure they do." Isaac stopped talking when he realized he merely placated. It had been so long since he'd had an honest conversation with anyone, he barely remembered how.

John leaned forward, one elbow in the middle of a note that read "Think." With his nearness came the smell of something, maybe cologne—earthy, spicy. "Do you write?"

"To be honest, not very well. I'd rather be reading than writing. I don't have much to say lately. Or maybe too much to say." Isaac now tapped nervously on the table. "I don't know."

The clatter of beer mugs announced Tommy's return. "Jesus, you two look like mournful gargoyles back here. Are we discussing the political climate or something?"

John laughed into his beer. "God, no. Anything but that."

Chapter Three

THE STEPS LEADING up to Isaac's apartment smelled of stomach contents. After another long day of prep, Isaac unlocked the door. Inside were a single couch, a heavy coffee table, and a few unpacked boxes. Isaac's bedroom had a twin bed and a closet with his clothes. There were no decorative items, and the only thing he'd bought so far for the kitchen had been a coffee machine. His empty apartment was a reminder of all he'd lost, so Isaac put on his running shoes and ran as soon as the sun went down.

Since moving to Lothos, he'd followed that identical pattern: work all day, run all night, and pretend to sleep. Luckily, prepping for classes kept his mind busy—although his phone still vibrated, unanswered, in desk drawers and coat pockets. When he fled Charleston, Isaac could have changed his number, bought a new phone, but he hadn't. Even if he never responded, he liked the familiarity of being called bad names—reminders of what he'd done to the people he once loved. Plus, it kept him abreast of Simon's wrath and if he might possibly find Isaac someday.

Into the warm night he went, a phantom hiding from light. He liked the ache of a good workout since it made him feel *something*, so he welcomed the steep hills of Southern Ohio and sprinted until muscles burned. It was coincidence that he ended up on College Green, but once there, it was hard to ignore the gold-glowing crowd.

How had he missed this? Surely, there had been an email, a flyer, something about a candlelight vigil. Isaac crept closer but drew back when he recognized familiar faces. He hid behind a tree, fearing they might shun his ignorance—his *otherness*. He wasn't one of them, and although he so far felt welcome, he would never be among those strangled by Hambden's collective tragedy. Isaac hung back in the shadows, covered in sweat, like an unwelcome interloper.

Twenty feet away, John stood near the front of the crowd, his arm around a crying Cleo. They were easy to spot, with Cleo's flaming red hair, John's pale skin and angular face. A group of close to fifty people stood beside Ellis Hall with their candles. A few students told stories with shaky voices. A tiny girl with long, black hair talked about her friend, Demi, "lost forever." The mention of Demi made Cleo hold John tighter. Alone, Isaac watched and waited until people started to vacate the area. Then, he ran home.

Dripping sweat onto the cheap linoleum, he chugged a bottle of water before sitting in front of his computer. Now desperately curious, he searched "Hambden University shooting." There were plenty of articles, some news stories. Most, though, were opinion articles about mental health and gun control, spouting the usual liberal versus conservative arguments he'd grown tired of after years of school shootings and no change.

Then, the headline, "Hero Teacher Tried to Talk Gunman Down." He clicked on the link, and there was a picture of John, Tommy right behind him, as always, both ducking away from what looked like a frenzy of media outside the tall white columns of Ellis Hall.

According to the article, the morning of June 6, creative writing student Chris Frank brought a .22 pistol to campus and started shooting. A couple quotes claimed he'd been "the all-American boy." No one could have expected him to shoot Dr. Abby Blake in the head and then keep shooting, shooting. Four more names of the dead: Dan Palmer, Russ Queensbrook, Demi Snyder, and Andrea Wilson. Then, there was John—John who, apparently, stood up in the midst of the shooting and stared Chris Frank in the face. John who, based on a grainy photo probably taken on a cell phone, had stood there, hands raised, when Chris pressed a gun to his neck.

"Jesus." Isaac wondered at the steel resolve it must have taken to just stand there and wait to catch a bullet. No way could Isaac have done that, no matter how dark his recent days. Isaac didn't want to die; did John? Were heroes people with death wishes? Did they want glory? Or did heroes possess some instinct to save other people that the majority of humanity lacked?

Whatever the reason, John Conlon hadn't died that day in June. No, instead of shooting John, Chris Frank had taken his own life. The horror had ended in little more than two minutes: two minutes that echoed and replayed across College Green over and over for everyone who'd been there.

The media had called John a hero: "the Hambden hero." In an interview, though, he'd crushed all their hopes of making him America's darling. He'd said, "If I was really a hero, six people wouldn't be fucking dead." How disappointing for the journalists. Looking at John—the grown man with an angel face—they'd probably thought they'd struck gold. They finally had a handsome hero. They could plaster his face everywhere, take the focus off the gun control debate, have a real story, and even better: John was gay! Minorities rejoice! Instead, he'd ducked their inquiries and sneered at the word "hero."

John didn't look like a hero. He looked like a college kid trying on adult clothes. He was too skinny and his hair too messy. His presence exuded an enigmatic mix of liveliness and quiet melancholy. Isaac couldn't picture John's delicate hands grabbing for a gun. He couldn't picture John's frail form tackling anybody. In fact, John Conlon seemed the more likely sort to end up shot. But he'd lived. He'd stood up to a shooter, talked to him, and the shooter had gone down.

Isaac hesitated before clicking the video. He hated feeding into the horror, but...

Warning: Graphic Content.

He could tell, by the angle, this was from where all the still images of John and Chris had been pulled. This was the shaky cell phone video taken by some terrified coed. He heard the harried breath, the quiet whimpers. In front of the camera, Chris walked around, shouting, gun in his hand. Nothing about him said murderer.

Then, John.

John went from holding the bleeding, broken body of a young woman to standing, his hands red. He held those blood-soaked hands out to Chris Frank and spoke, quietly. Impossible to miss Tommy in the background, holding Cleo, watching as his best friend was about to be destroyed. Gun now pressed to the center of John's neck, he kept talking until, suddenly, Chris put the gun to his own head and pulled the trigger. Everyone screamed, but John just stood there, staring at the corpse at his feet.

Isaac paused the video on John. Dark curls covered his face, and Isaac wanted to go back in time, brush the hair away, and wrap John in a hug. He wanted to look into John's green eyes and simultaneously yell "thank you" and "I am so angry with you." He at least wanted to wash the blood from John's hands.

It was no wonder they'd lost faculty, no wonder they couldn't find candidates to hire. Who would want to walk over old bloodstains? Who would want to remember the crack of gunfire across College Green? Isaac hadn't even been there, but he still felt sick. Hambden University was indeed haunted, but for Isaac, it was the perfect place to hide.

Chapter Four

WITH STUDENTS BACK and classes starting the following day, Isaac attended his first faculty meeting with Meeks at the helm. He knew the gist of how these things went, having been an English Department head himself for seven years at Broad College in Charleston before—well, before everything went to hell.

Usually, there were boring discussions of administrative tasks and vague talks about "goals." After all his morbid research into the shooting, Isaac expected this particular faculty meeting to be different, though. He expected his coworkers to relive the shooting, bemoan the absence of Dr. Abby Blake, who'd been at Hambden for over a decade before Chris Frank had shot her in the head. Instead, her replacement, Meeks, discussed code of conduct as if nothing horrible had happened.

Isaac needed to talk to John. More than talk, really; he wanted to lock the guy in a basement to ensure he never did something foolhardy again. This protectiveness over an almost stranger was unusual for Isaac, but there was no use questioning its existence. Already, John inspired in Isaac a need to shield, like a wolf protecting its cub. *Mess with him; mess with me.* Maybe because he looked so frail, or maybe because Isaac couldn't get the image of John with a gun to his throat out of his head.

They sat across from each other in the circle of desks and chairs, arranged in the middle of a large classroom on

Ellis's third floor. Tommy was to John's right and Cleo to his left. Slouched in his seat, John resembled a high school cool kid—the one who smoked cigarettes and took virginities. It was the hair that did it, added that touch of devil-may-care, along with the full mouth and hooded gaze. Cleo leaned to the side and wrote something in John's notebook. He read and mouthed, "No." Tommy whispered until John leaned closer, heads almost touching, and smiled.

"Now, I know we've been through a lot together," Meeks said, voice suddenly louder as if she knew Isaac hadn't been paying attention. "We all miss Abby and Demi. We need to lean on each other in this difficult time. We need to seek comfort in each other—but not too much comfort, if you get my meaning. You all remember what happened to Dr. Lancaster and Ms. Brown. Just because people are dead doesn't mean rules go out the window."

Isaac tried to swallow down his shock over her insensitivity, but no one else seemed surprised. Apparently, Meeks wore callous well.

She crossed her arms over her business suit, worn at the elbows. "We do still have counselors in place for students who need them—and faculty too. Those services are free for all of you. You've been trained to look for warning signs. If you think a student is having trouble, report it immediately, and—"

John's deep voice interrupted. "What's that going to accomplish? You want us to throw kids off campus if they seem twitchy?" He glared at her, waiting, and she glared back. No love lost between these two, evidently.

"No," Meeks said. "Just trying to be aware."

Isaac bit the insides of his cheeks and frowned around futility.

After the meeting, Isaac had to chase John out to College Green—the guy moved so fast from the classroom and down the steps. John had really long legs, so Isaac took a few jogging steps to catch up. "Hey, John."

He stopped walking and smiled. "Remember how to teach yet?"

"Not in any way."

John seemed so happy, gazing up at Isaac. He almost hated to ruin it.

"You were relieved I didn't know anything about the shooting."

As expected, John's face fell.

"Hambden hero."

John tucked some hair behind his ear, but a breeze immediately blew the strands free, along with a whiff of John's scent. "Someone's been googling."

Isaac stepped a little closer so people passing couldn't hear. "I know you don't think you're a hero, but you are. What you did was incredibly brave."

John exhaled loudly through his nose and closed his eyes. When he opened them, dark in the dim morning light, his gaze studied the brick sidewalk in the direction of downtown. "Coffee?"

They walked side by side to a coffee shop on Union called Donkey. The walls were painted dark brown to give the appearance of wood, while the floor was bright cedar. Everywhere floated the scent of coffee beans. They both ordered tall French roasts at John's insistence—"It's the best coffee outside my kitchen"—and sat on opposite ends of a long, purple couch. With one knee pulled up, John might as well have been lounging around at home. Isaac sipped the scalding coffee and winced at its strength.

John snorted. "You'll only be wide awake for a couple days."

"No kidding."

"Chris came to my office the week before it happened."

John's change in topic was even more shocking than the coffee.

"I knew something was wrong, but it was finals week, and I was so fucking busy. Too busy to listen." He sipped from his huge mug and stared at the floor.

"Do you blame yourself?"

He shrugged. "I don't know."

"You couldn't have known."

"No. No one expects…that. Maybe we should, though."

Isaac wrapped his palms around his scalding mug. "What did you say to him that day on College Green?"

"I don't remember."

"Liar."

John smiled and hid behind his hair. Isaac was beginning to wonder if he kept it long solely for that purpose.

"He was a good writer. Chris. Really good." He poked and tugged on a frayed couch cushion. "Of course, nobody's going to remember that now."

"You will."

John cleared his throat. "Why did you come here for work anyway? From what I've heard from Meeks, we couldn't get qualified faculty within twenty miles of this place. What are you, an ambulance chaser?"

"No." There was so much he could have said about his old life, his own tragedies. He could have been open to John as John was being open with him. Instead, he shrugged and said, "I just didn't know."

John lifted his other leg onto the couch and practically curled into a pretzel. "How did you not know? Been living under a rock?"

Keep it vague. "I was busy dealing with personal things."

"Personal things. Sounds very hush-hush. Mob put a price on your head?"

Isaac thought of his cell phone. The constant texts and calls from Simon had stopped recently, but that didn't mean anything was resolved. The quiet was more warning than relief. He sucked in a breath when John snapped his fingers in front of his face.

"Oh, my God, the mob *did* put a price on your head. How much? I could really use the extra cash."

Isaac laughed. "No. No, I'm sorry. I think this coffee is melting my brain."

"It's supposed to have the opposite effect."

To distract any and all attention from himself, Isaac said the first thing that came to mind. "Is Tommy in love with you?"

John's eyes widened. "Shit, man, uh, no. I mean, he's straight. He loves the chicks. We love each other like brothers do."

"He seems worried about you."

He leaned his head back against the couch. "Well, I did almost use my neck to catch a bullet last year, and Tommy had to sit there and watch. I assume that fucked him up a bit."

Isaac replayed the images of that day in his head again and shivered, suddenly cold.

John put his hand on his knee and gave it a quick, friendly squeeze. "See, 'don't be awkward.' Totally failing today."

"You're fine."

"That's what all the boys say." He waggled his dark eyebrows.

Isaac sputtered around a sip of coffee. Not a dull moment with John Conlon.

Chapter Five

THE FIRST WEEK of classes was arduous, simply because it had been ages since Isaac had worked with inexperienced writers. He was so accustomed to working with students who knew the craft. Teaching basic composition and working with—as predicted—business students who didn't know the correct use of a comma made his face burn.

And he was lonely. God, was he lonely.

At home, his cell phone again vibrated wherever he chose to keep it hidden. Cleo was the only person at Hambden who had his phone number. She had forced him out of his lonely, awful house one night to see her sing at a place next door called Crocodile Lounge. He'd even enjoyed himself a little. In her skintight black satin dress, Cleo had reminded him of a lounge singer from some noir film. Her voice reminded him of Billie Holiday.

When Friday rolled around, Isaac decided it was finally time to indulge. There was one gay bar in the area, and it was outside Lothos city limits. He did away with his usual tucked-in, Southern attire and went for a black button-down and jeans instead—although the boat shoes went along like a second skin. He drove himself to the Cave at ten p.m. and found it as billed: a dark and seedy place with no windows. Already, music blasted from the speakers, and drag queens mingled with the dancing crowd. From where he stood, most of the patrons were a bit younger than him, but he didn't see any college kids, at least. Not yet. They would probably arrive closer to midnight, as was the way of the young and fabulous, but he hoped to be long gone by then.

Isaac ordered a beer and ignored the eyes sizing him up—for the moment. He enjoyed the anonymity. In Charleston, he had rarely hit up the gay scene for fear of being recognized. He couldn't have afforded the scandal. In Ohio, he knew no one, not really, so he had nothing to fear—he thought. With his luck, he really should have expected the worst.

He caught sight of John in the mirror behind the bar.

Isaac immediately ducked to his right where he could just vaguely see John, but he was fairly certain John couldn't see him. Admirers greeted the handsome young professor with hugs and cheek kisses. There appeared to be an entire table of friends waiting for the guy, all dressed up, as was John, actually. Dark skinny jeans and a black velvet suit coat complemented his pale skin, and he'd left his usual Converse at home in exchange for shiny dress shoes.

One of the men jumped the table and dragged a smiling John away—even closer to Isaac, who ducked farther. They leaned against a nearby wall together, the tall blond with a ponytail looming large as they spoke. He grabbed onto the back of John's hair and pulled until John leaned his head back, and the blond nibbled down his jaw.

"They're not together." The bartender, of the huge and hunky variety, dried his hands behind the bar. "I think Adam's just glad to see him."

Isaac had to lean closer and yell over the music. "I'm sorry?"

"The sexy twink you've been checking out in the mirror. His name's John."

He'd definitely been caught looking, but he didn't have to lie. "Oh, he's not my type."

The bartender laughed. "John is everyone's type!"

That certainly seemed the case. In the reflection, John had already abandoned "Adam." A tall queen led him to the dance floor, where John moved his feet and hips in perfect synchronicity beneath the throbbing colored lights. For an English nerd, John sure knew how to move.

"You from around here?" the bartender asked, one meaty forearm resting near Isaac's beer.

Isaac returned his hungry gaze. "New in town." This was more Isaac's speed. He'd always had a thing for topping tough guys in bed.

"Welcome. I'm going to name your tab 'Greek' since you look like you climbed down from Olympus." He winked. "Next round's on me."

Isaac lifted his beer in salute, used to the attention. He might hate himself most days, but he knew how he looked. He knew guys liked the blond hair–blue eyes thing, along with his tall runner's body. He never had trouble finding lovers; case in point, the busy bartender... and the man with the close-cropped black hair across the bar.

Barely five words were exchanged before Isaac found himself and his dark stranger in the alley behind the Cave. They weren't the only ones, although they found a modicum of privacy behind a stack of empty kegs. The stranger's mouth tasted like the burn of alcohol, and he smelled like too much cologne. But he was good-looking— and talented on his knees.

Isaac came in less than three minutes and felt awful immediately. After buckling up, he walked away and didn't look back. He drove home to Lothos. In the shower, he turned the water on hot as it would go and took off his clothes. He stepped under the burning stream until his skin ached, scrubbing and scrubbing. Exhausted, he fell asleep face-first on the couch that'd come with the place. It smelled like stale smoke.

For the first time in a week, he dreamed of Elizabeth. She stood in his kitchen, naked, poking holes in her stomach with a knife until blood gushed from between her legs, and Isaac woke screaming.

He didn't know what time it was and didn't care. He pulled on his running shorts and shoes and escaped into the night. He hated living in a haunted house, so he ran and ran until he found himself lost in the nice neighborhoods outside of campus. Lost again—always lost. At the realization, he bent over, hands on his knees, and sobbed.

As he fell to the ground, he heard his name.

His vision fuzzy with tears, he would have recognized that hair anywhere.

John knelt and reached out his hand. "Isaac? Hey, what happened? What's wrong?"

Isaac fell forward into his arms, and under the force of his weight, John tumbled backward onto the pavement. Isaac hugged him close, sweat-soaked face against the side of his neck, but John didn't smell right. He didn't smell like his usual bouquet but like a dirty club and alcohol and sex. He smelled a lot like sex.

"It's okay," John whispered. "Whatever it is; it's okay. Why don't you come to my house for a bit?"

"No, no." Isaac pressed away from John and leaned back on his heels. "I should be alone."

"No one should be alone when they're crying." John stood and brushed his hands off on his jeans before reaching out to Isaac. "Come on."

Miraculously, they were only a few houses down from John's place. He eventually guided Isaac to his feet and walked him, hand around his waist, up the sidewalk and all the way to his living room. He made Isaac sit and then made him tea.

As John handed him a steaming mug, Isaac noticed the clock read 3:30 a.m. John sat on the edge of an ottoman in front of him.

"What were you doing out walking so late?"

John licked his top lip and smiled like the answer should be obvious. "Uh, I was…"

"You got laid."

"Right. Yeah."

"What cologne do you wear?"

He slurped his tea. "I don't."

Isaac ignored his hot beverage. "You have a smell."

"Oh, maybe witch hazel. I use it on my skin."

Isaac stared blankly at the floor.

"You want to talk about it?" John tipped his head toward the front door.

Isaac knew he could tell John the truth without fear of judgment, just say, *I am a gay man who spent my whole life closeted and married to a woman, and I don't know what I'm doing in Ohio. Please, help.* In reality, he said, "I got divorced about a year ago. Elizabeth and I were married for over ten years. It was bad, and I left my last job because of it. Lost my life, lost my family."

John leaned back. "Shit."

"I ran away. Here. I don't think Elizabeth even knows where I am. Nobody from my old life does, not that they would miss me."

"Isaac, I'm sorry."

He trembled as the sweat dried on his skin, and John must have noticed, because he grabbed a nearby afghan and threw it over him.

"I'll make it stink," Isaac said.

"I can wash it." He adjusted the blanket so it hugged Isaac's shoulders and tucked beneath his chin, not noticing or caring when his fingertips brushed lightly against Isaac's collarbone and neck.

Isaac shivered some more and set down the untouched tea. "What happened last year, didn't it mess you up?"

John rolled his eyes. "Well. Yeah."

"You don't seem it. You walk around campus like this bright light, and everyone loves you."

"Everyone does *not* love me."

"Sonya Meeks?" Isaac tugged the afghan tighter as though the mention of her name gave the room added chill.

"Sonya and I have known each other a long time. We just are the way we are."

Isaac considered his next question, wondering if it gave too much away or said much too little. "How did you keep going after it happened?"

"I don't know." John chuckled, and soon, they were both laughing in the sick, twisted way broken people do. "The nights are the worst."

"For me too," Isaac said. "I need to be doing something to fill the quiet. I had so much before the divorce. I did so much, and now, it's all gone. Sometimes, I wish I could go back and start all over."

John laughed again but stopped suddenly. "Sorry, I'm not laughing at you. I just feel like I'm talking to myself." He turned the mug forward and back between his palms while chewing his bottom lip. When he didn't speak, the only sound became that of newly arrived rain outside.

Isaac watched John's face change. His brow warped into wrinkles, and he sucked both his lips into his mouth.

"What is it?" Isaac asked. "Should I go?"

"No." John put his hand on Isaac's knee. When Isaac remained seated, he pulled it back. "I was thinking of something for you to do. I'm the faculty advisor for the Hambden literary magazine. My star editor, Janelle—she has this idea. I haven't run it by Meeks yet, but Janelle wants the theme of this year's magazine to be the shooting."

"Oh" was Isaac's only justifiable response.

John scratched at his scalp, curls going into further disarray. "Yeah, I know, it's ballsy. And possibly insane, but it feels like everyone's trying to forget it happened— the school, Sonya, even Tommy. Janelle thought it might be nice if there was a place where students could submit poems or short stories in memory of the people we lost or even just about that day. I would obviously vet everything. Would you want to help? You could be my second-in-command."

Isaac sat up straighter. "Really?"

John shrugged. "Get you back in the game. We meet Tuesday nights."

"Amazingly enough, my Tuesday nights are free."

John reached out his hand. "Then, it's settled."

Isaac shook it, enveloping John's smaller hand in his own. Just the idea, the mere suggestion, of having something creative to do made his chest feel warm. Surely, the warmth had nothing to do with John's proximity or the way his eyes crinkled at the edges when he smiled.

As if silently agreed, they both stood and walked toward the front door. John pulled his cell phone from his back pocket. "Let me get your digits."

Isaac shared his phone number but paused in the foyer by the library. "Can I read one of your books?"

John looked up from under his brows. "They're really gay."

Isaac laughed at both the skepticism and irony. "I don't mind."

Taking off his suit coat, John walked past him into the library. He tossed his jacket on the desk and ran a finger over book bindings before pulling one free. "Here."

Isaac took the proffered book and recognized the gold circle on the front. "You won the Newbery Medal?"

John looked away, cheeks red. "I told you I'm a better writer than teacher." John shoved his hands in his pockets, and Isaac had the sudden, irrational fear of leaving the safe, cozy space. He did a slow circle until a mounted album caught his eye amidst all the other music posters: James Taylor, *Sweet Baby James*. He made a beeline.

"Is that signed?"

"Yeah. I've seen James live twice, met him once." John ran a fingertip across the frame, dusty at the bottom.

"He's one of my favorites. I've never..." Isaac stumbled over his own excitement. "I've always wanted to see him. There just never seemed to be an opportunity. What was he like?"

"Funny. Friendly." John's cheekbones picked up light from the hallway and glowed. "He tells these stories, and it feels like he's talking right to you—like you're in an empty room together. Then, during intermission, he sits on stage, and you can run up there and have him sign album covers, breasts, whatever."

"James Taylor signed your breast?"

John giggled—a loud sound that echoed into the foyer and back. "I did have to restrain myself from rubbing all over him. I think he was my first crush."

Isaac lifted the book. "Your author bio says you like 'old-people music.' Is this what you mean?"

"Pretty much. My dad raised me on it."

"You don't dance like a fan of old-people music."

One of John's brows lifted. "When have you seen me dance?"

Isaac scrambled for an answer that didn't include the Cave. "Well, you did moonwalk into Joe's Pub."

John yawned. "Oh, right."

Isaac turned and almost ran into the doorframe. "I should go."

"Are you going to be all right?"

Isaac nodded, and even if it was a lie, John made the lie easier.

Before he could leave, John put a hand on his shoulder. "I'll text you so you have my number. If you need anything, just call, okay? I'm serious. Any time of day."

A handshake didn't feel like enough, so Isaac gave John a quick and enthusiastically reciprocated hug.

After a reminder on directions, Isaac found the strength to jog home through the rain. When he got there, he still smelled witch hazel. Out of habit, he checked his phone, but no angry messages awaited him—just a quick text from John.

"Call me, fucker" with a thumbs-up emoji.

Isaac hadn't been so charmed by someone in years.

ISAAC TAUGHT TWO composition classes Monday morning, which he floated through in a sort of idiotic haze. He couldn't get his brain to operate, and he hoped the students didn't notice. Maybe it was the Monday funk—or maybe this was who he was now, the stereotypical absent-minded professor. Tommy and John invited him to lunch, and their friendly shenanigans kept him entertained, especially when they fought about college football. They were the two stooges, and the fond way John smiled at Isaac made him wonder if the guys were secretly interviewing him to be stooge number three.

The rain from Friday night stretched into Tuesday. Between three and four p.m., many of the teachers held office hours, including Isaac. He stood in the open doorway of his office and pretended to skim a pamphlet about the Hambden University MFA program when he actually observed the scene down the hall.

Visibly, John had been caught in the storm. He shook fistfuls of raindrops on the carpet while Tommy tried to stay away from the watery barrage. Wet, John's hair reached all the way to his shoulders. He shoved soaked strands back over his forehead and said something that made Tommy laugh.

Isaac dropped the pamphlet he pretended to read at the sound of Cleo's voice. "He is ridiculously attractive, isn't he?"

"You scared me."

"Sorry, Dr. Twain."

"No, it's fine." He tried to catch his breath. "Just surprised me. What did you say?"

"John. He's a dreamboat." She looked back toward the soaked creative writing teacher. "He used to be more filled out before the summer, but he's still so cute. He has that skinny punk thing going on now, like he should be smoking expensive cigarettes with a British accent or something."

"Oh, I wasn't..." Panicked at her insinuation, Isaac shook his head.

"Oh, my God, that was so rude. I just assumed—the way you were looking at him." She hit herself lightly on the forehead. "Oh, Cleo."

"It's okay." He thought about spouting some lie—*I'm straight, I love women*—but didn't have the energy.

She put her hands by her mouth and imitated vomit with her hands, fingers moving from her lips toward the floor in a rainbow arc. "I say dumb things all the time. It's probably why I'm still single. Please don't be mad at me."

"I'm not." *Change the subject.* "Will you let me know when you sing again?"

She beamed, red lips matching her hair. "Yes! For sure."

A dripping John appeared, took Cleo's hand, and kissed it before playfully punching Isaac in the shoulder. "Ready for tonight?"

Isaac nodded and backed against the wall, away from John, as Meeks stuck her head from her office. "John. Isaac. Could I see you both for a second?"

John used his wet coat cuff to wipe water droplets from his lips and heaved a wary glance Isaac's way. Isaac just shrugged. They couldn't be in trouble for the literary magazine; no one even knew about the controversial theme—yet.

"Don't suppose you have a towel in there?" John asked.

"Don't suppose you have an umbrella?" She disappeared back into her office.

John sighed. "She loves me."

"I can tell," Isaac replied and followed John down the hall.

Meeks's office had zero personality, walls bare but for two diplomas and shelves with a few books. It felt cold. Isaac knew it had belonged to Meeks's predecessor, Abby Blake, who had died on College Green. Perhaps the emptiness was symbolic of Abby's absence, or perhaps Meeks was just empty inside, truly the cruel robot she appeared to be.

"Sit," Meeks said immediately and then spoke again. "Not you, John. I'd rather you not ruin my furniture."

He remained standing, arms crossed, so Isaac did, too, in solidarity. Even from where he stood, he could smell Meeks, the reek of cigarettes.

"The Ohioana Literary Festival is this weekend," she said. "And I'd like you both to attend on behalf of Hambden University."

"What?" John spat.

Meeks didn't even look up from a file on her desk. "John, you're going to be a featured speaker."

"Sonya, you know the kind of questions I'm going to get. It'll be a circus."

"Yes, that's why it's so last minute. We didn't want the media getting wind of your presence, although it's not as if they miss you."

Like water before a boil, Isaac felt the tension rising in John. His pale cheeks began to flush, and he curled his hands into fists. Maybe Isaac should speak up, diffuse the tension, but Isaac didn't know either John or Meeks well enough to guess at what might calm either of them. He kept his mouth shut.

John flipped wet curls from his face. "Handling the media was never my job."

"Clearly." She brushed at some lint on her dark dress pants. Her hair, as usual, clung to the back of her head in an angry bun. "Isaac, you're going with him as a watchdog. Make sure he behaves."

John scoffed and rolled his eyes.

"I'm sure he'd prefer Tommy," Isaac said.

"Yes, he would, but John and Tommy are like frat boys together. You're older and more responsible, from what I can tell. You're also a fresh face. Neutral. The sooner people forget about the past and move toward the future, the better, which is partially why John is speaking—to show he's alive and well and we're...that the school is still a place of higher education and not just the scene of a tragedy."

John crossed his arms and stomped one foot. "What if I don't want to go?"

"John." She rubbed her eyes. "I know you're young, but don't be a child."

"Then, don't treat me like one."

"Your presence will cause a stir at the Ohioana, but we can't let it get out of control. You're a *hero*, after all." She made it sound like a dig. "Isaac, I trust you'll keep things in order."

He could have offered promises and platitudes, but Isaac wasn't her trained dog. When he didn't speak, she moved on.

"Just do your job as a trusty emergency hire." She stood, physically closing the conversation. "You'll leave early Saturday morning. A day, a night, and you're both back on Sunday. I'm sure you can handle that. And I booked the last room, so I'm sorry, but you have to share."

Oh, hell, no.

Isaac wanted to protest about the single room. He could stay in another hotel maybe? There had to be one close by. He couldn't stay in the same room with John, not because something might happen but because...

Shit, something actually *might happen.*

The magnetic pull that was John Conlon only continued to grow stronger the more time they spent together, but all that was just fine and safe in public. Within the small confines of a hotel room, where Isaac might see John in cuddly pajamas, watch him brush his teeth, hear him snore? It was too intimate, too much, especially as sex-starved as Isaac felt. He was about to speak up when John grabbed his arm and pulled him into the hall.

John walked and seethed, his hair drying in Shirley Temple rings. "Who the fuck does she think she is?"

Isaac followed close behind. "I'm sorry?"

"Why are you sorry?"

"I don't know."

Tommy sat in John's office, reading a stack of papers. He looked up when they entered. "Why are flames shooting out of your eyes?"

"Fucking Meeks. She's sending me to Ohioana as a speaker."

Tommy's mouth dropped open, and he actually removed his thick glasses. "You can't go. You'll be mobbed."

"Isaac's my bodyguard."

"Well, he's got the build for it. Want me to go too?"

"No, you're not allowed." John peeled off his wet coat, revealing an equally soaked plaid shirt. "Apparently, we misbehave together."

"Tell me you're taking all your drugs with you."

"Yes." John gestured toward Isaac. "And thanks."

Tommy winced. "Sorry."

"Hey, I like drugs," Isaac said in an effort to ease the tension, and John sort of laughed. He at least made a sound between an amused snort and a cough.

"What are you speaking about anyway?" Tommy asked.

"I don't know. How not to get shot?" John covered his mouth.

Tommy stood quickly and put both hands on John's shoulders. "Okay, let's breathe."

John took a single deep breath before leaning the top of his head against Tommy's chest and hiding his face. His breath shook, and he sniffed, wiping at his eyes.

"Let it out, dude," Tommy whispered.

Again, Isaac felt the now familiar need to just *hug*. Instead, he rested his palm on John's upper back. "You got this," he said.

John lifted his head, cheeks wet with tears. "Yeah." He pressed both palms against his eyes. "Shit."

"Isaac, promise to take care of him?"

Suddenly, all the nerves about sharing a hotel room vanished because Isaac had a task. He had a function. He was needed, so he smiled. "Feed him liquor and punch the paparazzi? I'm on it."

John smiled, thank God. "Actually, maybe it's a good place to announce the literary magazine. Subversive but interesting. Meeks will be less likely to reject us if I've told the entire Ohio higher-ed community."

Tommy shook his head. "Naughty boy."

"We'll make the best of it, huh?"

Isaac muttered platitudes of agreement, and they spent the rest of their office hour debating the college Bowl Championship Series.

IN A THIRD-story classroom of Ellis Hall, they crammed together, the myriad members of Hambden University's literary magazine staff. Isaac had already met Janelle earlier. She'd been close with Demi and hadn't even hesitated to tell Isaac, "She died in my arms."

Janelle was the big brains behind the project and, according to John, a budding writer of the morbid and macabre. She looked the part. No bigger than five foot four, she had light eyes and wore lots of bracelets on her left wrist. Her black T-shirt had a picture of a vampire bunny rabbit, and her jeans were skintight, bottomed off by Converse—dead ringers for the ones John wore every day.

Despite her tiny voice, Janelle opened the discussion with strength and clarity. "We're all here because we want to remember the people who were murdered. Or we at least want to write about what happened." She pulled a notebook from her black bag as she talked and then looked at John. "I thought up a name, but..."

"But what?" John leaned back in a student-sized desk, slouching as usual with his skinny legs stretched in front of him like stilts.

"The name." She itched at the bracelets on her wrist. "People might not like it."

John shrugged. "In writing, if you haven't pissed someone off, you probably aren't doing it right."

Janelle tapped black-painted fingernails on the desk. "I want to call it *Being Frank*."

The room went silent. Kids stopped shifting in their seats.

When John didn't say anything, Isaac asked, "Why do you want to call it that?"

She focused her attention on him. "I know the magazine is in memory of the victims, but I guess I've been thinking, what did Chris Frank feel that day? Why did he do it, you know? Nobody got to ask him." She looked at John. "Did you ask him?"

All eyes turned to their professor.

"No," he said.

"I just think Chris should be remembered too," she continued and shrugged. "Maybe someone will even write about him."

A dark-skinned boy with tight curls gripped the front of his desk. He'd introduced himself earlier as Anthony. Not Tony but *Anthony*. "And 'being frank' means being honest, right? We need to be honest about what happened. Not just throw flowers on the altar out there but be real about how it feels to be back here after that day. Right, John?"

John ran his hands through his hair, already a mess. After his finger comb, he looked like a nervous madman. "I'm going to get in so much trouble for this. Isaac, what do you think?"

He thought he felt alive. He wanted to do a little jig in celebration of subversion, but calmly, he took a long, slow breath. "If you haven't pissed someone off..."

The two grown men stared at each other until John grinned.

"All right, honestly? You're my best students. I trust each of you, but we're going to get heat for this. There are going to be people who are very upset, especially with the name—but I'm willing to do this if you are. Especially if you think it'll help."

Janelle nodded.

A couple of the other kids looked nervous, but they eventually nodded, as well. Isaac felt a prickling in his spine that might be the birthing of his new life, especially when he made eye contact with John's glittering gaze.

"All right. We need to make a timetable, including the call for submissions." John paused. "Then, I need a drink."

SATURDAY MORNING, ISAAC lugged his bag up the hill from Union Street to John's house in a state of buzzing nerves. He liked John, of course, liked spending time with him, and the impromptu trip did get Isaac away from his lonely apartment. Some of his initial fears about sharing a hotel room had been forgotten. Isaac had talked himself out of any romantic affiliations with John because, for one thing, John wasn't even his type, even if he was charismatic and almost too beautiful to be real. Secondly, no way was Isaac jeopardizing his job, not now when the literary magazine had given him something to look forward to. Sharing a room with John would be fine— maybe fun. If Isaac was lucky, the sound of another person breathing nearby might even keep bad dreams at bay.

The sun had just barely risen above the edges of the Lothos city limits, washing the quiet, morning air in an orange tint. In the hills, away from downtown, the air smelled not of stale beer but of wet forest floors. John's porch light was on when he arrived, so he knocked twice and waited.

Tommy answered the door in a white T-shirt and boxers. "Isaac," he grumbled and wandered back into the house.

Isaac assumed he was to follow. He set his duffel bag in the foyer and walked inside. In the living room, Tommy fell back onto the couch and pulled a blanket over his head. From down the hall came the sound of John's voice. As Isaac neared a closed door he assumed led to the bedroom, he overheard the end of a conversation. In a completely different language.

Isaac leaned his ear against the door. He thought it was French: really fast, slightly agitated French. He recognized the word "Mama" but little else. There was also a lot of "no" going on.

Suddenly, the door swung open, and John ran into Isaac. "Shit!"

Isaac backed up. He felt his cheeks burn, guilty at being caught. "Sorry, I wasn't eavesdropping. Were you just speaking French?"

"Yeah, my mom is French."

"And incredibly hot," Tommy yelled from down the hall.

John rolled his eyes. "I look just like her. It's probably why he hangs out with me." He walked into the kitchen.

"You feeling okay?" Isaac asked because John looked tired and thinner than usual.

"Yeah." A black newsboy cap covered his dark hair, although errant curls escaped the back.

Okay, moving on. "I thought your family was in Wisconsin?"

"They are," John said.

"But your mom's French?"

"She's *from* France. She doesn't *live* in France. She met my dad when he was backpacking through Europe."

"Sounds like a movie," Isaac said.

Tommy remained hidden under blankets. "And how is the delightful Mrs. Conlon?"

"She misses me."

"Didn't you just spend the whole summer with your parents?" Isaac asked.

John looked up at him and hesitated for a second. "Yeah. Well." He pulled the cuffs up on his long-sleeved gray T-shirt and gave his tight jeans a tug as if they might fall off. "Do you want coffee for the road?"

"Sure."

"Tommy!" John yelled.

There was a muffled groan.

"Stop being hungover, and make Isaac coffee."

"But *you* make the best coffee," Tommy mumbled.

"But *I'm* still packing," John replied. "And make me your specialty."

More groaning but also the sound of shifting fabric.

"Give me five minutes," John said, walking toward the bathroom. "Do you mind driving for a little while? I'm not quite awake yet."

"Late night?" Isaac asked.

John seemed to consider but, instead of responding, just hummed and disappeared down the hall. A little while later, the two travelers headed to the garage while Tommy made unnecessary amounts of noise in John's kitchen. They were loading their bags into the trunk of a simple, red Toyota when Tommy came out bearing beverages.

"Don't look so grumpy. It's not like you're walking into the lion's den." John took the silver travel mugs and handed one to Isaac.

"I know." Tommy rubbed his eyes. "Be careful."

"Of what?" John asked.

Isaac thought the same.

"You sure you don't want me to come with you guys? I can be ready in twenty."

John opened the passenger door. "Meeks would just be pissed. Don't worry about it, man." John gave him a quick hug with a slap on the back. "See you tomorrow. We need to catch up on our ESPN."

"I know. Beginning of the semester sucks." Tommy turned and wandered back toward the garage door, shamelessly scratching his ass before throwing up a peace sign.

They climbed in and set their mugs in the cupholders. John pointed. "Mine is in the front. Yours is in the back. Don't confuse the two."

"Dare I ask why?" Isaac had to push the seat back to make room for his legs.

"Yours is coffee. Mine's a Bloody Mary."

Isaac put the car in reverse. "And Meeks thinks you act like a frat boy."

"I don't deny these claims." When he leaned his head against the headrest, his hat fell forward over his eyes.

Isaac followed the GPS on his phone away from Lothos and out to the highway, headed for Columbus, while John fiddled with the radio. They settled on scan, sticking with random songs and often debating their quality.

When James Taylor popped up, "Carolina in My Mind," John sang along. His singing voice was similar to his speaking voice: low, resonant, and lovely. The song tugged on Isaac's memory like grappling hooks until he had to change the channel.

"Hey, I liked that one."

Isaac kept his eyes on the road. "Not in the mood."

John yawned and stretched, his hair in his face now that the newsboy hat had tumbled into his lap. He scooped up Isaac's phone, ostensibly to check the GPS. "Simon texted."

Isaac snatched the phone away but set it gingerly in the cupholder as if a gentle follow-up could make John forget the momentary violence of his desperate grab.

John didn't apologize for touching his phone or acknowledge Isaac's psychotic response. He didn't even ask about Simon. He just said, "How soon until we get there?"

AT A BIG hotel and conference center on the outskirts of Columbus, Ohio, literary illuminati convened to learn, share, and bump egos. Isaac parked and opened his door, but John stayed planted in his seat, staring at the floor. "You okay?"

"Should be. Saw my shrink yesterday. Took my drugs. Living the pimp life."

Isaac smiled.

John pulled his newsboy cap snuggly onto his head, as if that would disguise his chiseled features—easily recognizable since most human beings didn't resemble fairy-tale nymphs. "Let's check in. We can drop our stuff in the room and start *mingling*."

"Wow, I've never thought of 'mingling' as a filthy word before," Isaac said. "Seriously, are you okay?"

John sighed. "Just keep up."

As they walked across the lobby, decorated in bright, modern colors and filled with geometric shapes—even the lime-green couches—John kept his head low, eyes focused on the ground. Isaac was the one who couldn't help but look around, because as soon as people saw John, recognized him, conversations stopped. People turned to look, cautiously, as if their stares did not scream volumes.

Whispers...

"That's the Hambden hero."

"John Conlon. Didn't expect to see him."

"Remember that shooting?"

Isaac wanted to scream at them; tell them to stop staring. Maybe he would make a good bodyguard, after all. He had to hurry to keep up with John, who although a bit shorter, seemed to be taking much longer strides. Keep up, indeed.

They rode the elevator to the ninth floor in silence. Isaac scrolled through words in his mind but thought of nothing useful to say. When they found their room, John swiped the keycard across the door. Inside was a lot like the lobby: too bright and filled with hip, ugly shades of orange, yellow, and baby blue. John tossed his suitcase on one of the double beds and stood by the window, staring out through gauzy curtains.

"Are you okay?"

"Fuck, Isaac, can you stop asking me that?"

Despite the venomous words, John's tone was that of piteous desperation—so Isaac took pity. He said, "It's just that, you know, your sex appeal knows no bounds." He unzipped his suitcase and took out a toiletry bag.

John looked back at him. "What?"

Isaac shrugged. "Everyone was staring at you because you're hotter than a skillet at breakfast." He didn't bust out the Southern expressions much, but this one was worth it, because a John smile, brighter than thirty suns, illuminated their ghastly hotel room.

"You're ridiculous," he said.

Isaac pulled out his toothbrush but before going to freshen up asked, "You know you can do this, right?"

John's shoulders slumped when he put his hands in his pockets. "Not without you, apparently."

"Well, I'm here, and I'm not going anywhere."

John sat on the edge of his bed. Isaac joined him without hesitation. They leaned against each other and stared at Isaac's toothbrush.

OF ALL THE meeting rooms in the conference hall that night, Isaac suspected the only one full to bursting was John's. Isaac stood to the side, and no matter how much they'd joked, he was ready to jump in front of his friend, protect him, especially when John's pale hands tapped the podium as he spoke, and people lifted cell phones to take pictures.

John started by discussing shy creative writing students and how to bring them out of their shells. He looked different in front of a crowd. It had to be the tie. Isaac had never seen him wear a tie. Granted, it was a silly tie with broad, diagonal rainbow stripes, but it was a *tie*, although John hadn't dressed up his jeans or Converse shoes. He stood taller too. John had a tendency to curl in on himself, but this must be "teacher John," who stood with his shoulders back, eyes shining with enthusiasm.

Unaware of who Isaac was, people whispered around him. There were the repeated mutterings from earlier, hushed pronouncements of *shooting, Hambden, hero.* One woman said, "I thought he'd be taller." Isaac ignored them as best he could, focusing as John moved on to talk about literary magazines and how useful they could be to bolster a young writer's confidence. Surprisingly, he didn't mention anything about *Being Frank.* Maybe he wasn't ready for the outcry.

He opened the floor for questions, which Isaac immediately knew was a bad idea, even before the first man raised his hand and asked, in a loud, clear voice, "How do you prevent school shootings?"

The room hushed.

John ran a hand through his dark hair. The change in his expression wouldn't be noticeable unless you knew him. Isaac knew him well enough, and his own shoulders tensed when he realized John was angry. He pretty much mimicked his long-ago comments to the media. "If I knew the answer to that, five of my students wouldn't be fucking dead."

Several people gasped.

"Okay." Isaac pushed away from the wall and hurried to John, his hand on his lower back. "That's enough questions. Thank you for your attentiveness. I think we could all use a drink."

Faint agreements preceded the mass exodus.

Meanwhile, John walked over to the window and leaned his forehead against the glass. "Jesus, what am I, twelve?" Air puffed out in a white cloud across the window. "I'm an idiot."

"That guy was an idiot," Isaac said. "Let me buy you a beer. Or maybe something stronger."

Isaac led the way, doing his best to shield John from unwanted attention—difficult, if not impossible. If only John wasn't so recognizable. If only he hadn't just dropped the f-bomb in a room full of teachers.

Different from the brightly lit foyer, the bar was made of dark wood and the walls a deep shade of green. Already, other teachers hovered over cloudy martinis. Isaac leaned his elbows on the bar and ordered two whiskeys, neat.

"It was a good presentation," Isaac said. What else could he say?

"It's recycled. I've used it before."

"You didn't mention *Being Frank*."

John talked to the bar. "It doesn't belong to the world. It belongs to us. Felt too personal."

The female bartender, dressed in a tuxedo vest and white shirt, returned with two rocks glasses filled with liquid amber. Isaac moved to hand over some cash, but she shook her head. "Your drinks are free. The gentleman at the end of the bar bought your first round."

John loosened his tie as they both turned to look. A handsome silver fox lifted his glass in toast before coming closer. He reached his hand right past Isaac to John. "Paul Harvey with Ohio State. Welcome to Buckeye country."

"You know I went to Wisconsin, right?"

"In that case..." Paul moved to grab John's drink, and John snatched it away.

"Too late. You already bought. Sht. This is Isaac."

Paul barely wasted a glance. "You're even better-looking than your pictures."

Isaac wanted to kidnap John and rush him back to their room, but John just smirked. "You're laying it on pretty thick for seven o'clock, Paul."

"You're a popular commodity around here. I didn't want to send mixed messages and miss my chance." He put his hand over John's. "Let me take you to dinner in the city."

"That sounds just about perfect, Paul Harvey from Ohio State." John finished his drink. "Isaac, you mind if I ditch you for a bit?"

Isaac fought the urge to grab onto him and hold—to say, *Stay with me. Stay with me.* "No problem," he said.

Maybe it didn't sound as convincing as he'd hoped, because John put his hand on Paul's forearm. "Could you give us a second?"

Paul nodded and stepped back to his earlier perch down the bar.

"I don't have to go," John said.

"I'm supposed to be protecting you. What if he's a serial killer?"

John looked around Isaac at Paul. "Serial killers don't wear tweed."

"John."

"You could come with. Play cock block."

"And watch the old man make heart eyes at you all night?" Isaac wanted to punch something—Paul maybe. "Doesn't sound like my idea of a good time."

John stood and straightened his tie. "I won't be out late."

"Be as late as you want." He saluted with fake nonchalance.

"And miss our slumber party? Never." John grinned. "Don't have too much fun without me."

"I'd say ditto, but..." He tipped his head toward Paul.

Isaac only stayed to finish his drink before going upstairs, where he ordered room service: a surprisingly delicious chicken quesadilla of which his nerves allowed him to eat barely half. What was the matter with him? John was a grown man, and Isaac wasn't *actually* his bodyguard—or his father, for that matter. He had no claim. None.

Around ten, he told himself he was tired and prepared for bed. He tried not to snoop as he brushed his teeth, but it was hard not to, with all the orange prescription bottles poking from the top of John's toiletry bag: Zoloft, Klonopin, and Prazosin. Isaac knew Zoloft was for depression. Klonopin was an anxiety drug. He'd never heard of the last one, though.

He spit into the sink and rinsed his mouth and toothbrush and turned off the light. He lay in his double bed, nearest the door, and continued reading John's book—the second of John's books. Isaac had finished the first one in two days, giving up sleep in exchange for literary brilliance. It was no wonder John won awards, and with every word, Isaac understood the man more and more. He'd known plenty of authors and read their works, but not one flayed themselves open on the page quite as fully as John Conlon. His emotional honesty was as impressive as it was terrifying.

Isaac dozed lightly, the book open on his chest, when he heard the lock click open. John tumbled in, hair and tie askew. He bounced onto his back next to Isaac.

"Somebody looks drunk."

John folded his hands across his stomach, with his eyes shut. "Ding-ding."

"You do realize this isn't your bed."

"Meh."

Isaac put the book down and rested on his elbow. "How was Paul?"

"Handsy."

"I'll bet." Isaac brushed the front of John's hair with his fingertips, pushing dark pieces back over his forehead. It was a friendly gesture, nothing more, just getting the poor guy's hair out of his face.

John's eyes opened midcaress. He made a pleased little squeak and smiled when his gaze focused on Isaac. Isaac ran his thumb over John's bottom lip, just to feel it—soft, as expected. It was merely a tactile experiment, because John wasn't his type; he really wasn't, and they were coworkers, so—

Isaac leaned forward and kissed him.

John froze for a second before reciprocating the kiss, one of his hands pressing to the back of Isaac's head. John opened his mouth, practically begging for Isaac's tongue, and Isaac gave and gave until they were panting into each other's mouths, and Isaac knew John tasted like whiskey and felt like biting into a damn sun-warmed peach.

Then, with a jerk, John pulled back and cussed before jumping from the bed and pointing. "You're straight."

Isaac stood, too, on the opposite side of the room. "I'm so sorry."

"Bisexual?"

He shook his head. "Gay."

"But you were married to a woman for, like, ever."

"I told you the divorce was bad."

"No shit." John buried both his hands in his hair, lips parted and, frankly, shimmering with Isaac's spit. "Oh, my God, you can't be attracted to me."

"Okay."

"People have gotten fired for this, and I need my job."

"John, calm down. I'm sorry. It won't happen again. I don't know what I was thinking." And it was so true.

Isaac never went for guys who looked like John, but maybe he'd transcended that? Maybe he was so insane over the entirety of John Conlon—mind, soul, spirit—that the feminine physicality was just another thing to now fawn over? No, this was not okay. He had to stop, just stop. He was too old for infatuation. "I'm sorry," he said again.

John pressed his lips together and looked like he might cry. He pointed to the bathroom. "I'm going to wash up, and you're going to bed."

Isaac intercepted with a hand in the way but still kept a careful distance. "I'm really sorry, John."

He whistled, low and quick. "Look. I kissed back, but I don't want things to be weird. Can we make sure things aren't weird? I like you a lot, and I've lost too many people lately."

"You won't lose me."

"And if you think we're done talking about your marriage, we're not. I'm just too fucking tired to get into it right now."

"Maybe you'll forget about it by morning?"

John chuckled, once, loudly. "You're not that lucky."

ISAAC WOKE TO the sight of John's bare back. He was across the room, thankfully, in his own bed, but the early morning sunlight made him glow. John was curled away on his side; the knobs of his spine stuck out like thimbles. Lacking a single freckle, his skin had possibly never seen the sun. John rolled onto his back, stretched. For a full-grown man, he was thin and small and practically hairless. How old was he anyway? Isaac had never thought to ask.

He pretended not to watch, keeping only one eye open as John arched his lower back off the bed and groaned. Isaac could probably wrap his large hands all the way around that waist and wouldn't mind testing the theory. John rubbed his eyes and reached blindly above his head, grabbing a small red container. The mouth guard made a wet smacking sound as he dislodged it from his top teeth and put it away. When he finally opened his eyes, Isaac closed his and feigned sleep. He didn't want to do this talking thing yet—possibly, not ever.

He heard the shift of blankets, followed by the click of the hotel phone. John whispered, "Room service? Could we get coffee please? Oh, and do you have bagels? Two bagels with cream cheese, thanks." The sound of John's feet on the floor and water running in the bathroom preceded a body landing on Isaac's bed, and Isaac sat up, surprised.

John sat next to him, wearing plaid pajama pants and a Wisconsin hoodie. After having learned they were to share a hotel room, Isaac had considered such an adorable outcome. The reality was much cuter than his imagination had invented.

John showed his teeth in a silly grin. "Morning."

"Shit." Isaac ran his hand over his chin and realized he needed a shave. "Morning."

"Coffee's on the way."

"Mm." He moved up next to John, and they sat there, silent, backs against the headboard. "How'd you sleep?"

"Fine. I was drunk."

"Your hair is preposterous."

John reached up and tugged it. "Goblins come in the night and tie it in knots." He touched his mouth. "And I have whisker burn."

A knock on the door saved Isaac further embarrassment.

Like a servant in a big house, John poured their coffees—both black—and took a huge bite of bagel. "You want some?" he asked between chews. Even with half-masticated food on full display, Isaac wanted to kiss him.

He feigned disinterest. "You make it look so appetizing."

"I'm hungover. I require sustenance." He climbed back onto Isaac's bed on his knees and kept eating, drinking. "So why did you marry a woman?"

"Oh, Jesus."

"He's not here right now."

Isaac took a big sip of coffee. "He's everywhere."

"Oh, I see. Religion made you do it?"

"No, Catholicism made me do it. Maybe. I don't know." He rubbed sleep boogers from the corners of his eyes. "I was young, and I loved her."

John settled in against the headboard, nesting himself low like a bear prepping for hibernation. "Tell me about her."

"Seriously?"

"Yep, we're doing this."

"Elizabeth." He hadn't said her name in months, and the name tasted strange in his mouth. "She was an anthropologist. We met in grad school at Auburn. She didn't look like anyone else. Unique—kind of like you, I guess. She had this short, spikey hair and fragile features, like Tinker Bell. I did love her, and my parents were conservative Southern Catholics."

John swallowed a huge hunk of bagel. "But you already knew you were gay?"

"I'd only been with one guy before, in undergrad at Vanderbilt."

"I remember kissing a girl when I was thirteen and thinking: 'Wow, that was gross.'"

Isaac shook his head. "Nothing was that clear for me—not until later. Elizabeth was doing all these archaeological digs around the world, and I had to stay home and work. It started innocently enough, just browsing websites. Then, I went to a gay club and..."

"Found your people."

Isaac opened his mouth and closed it, opened it again. "I don't want to tell you any more right now, because I don't want you to hate me."

John nudged him with his elbow. "I won't hate you."

"Everyone else does."

"That's some heavy shit."

He leaned forward and grabbed his own bagel off the tray. *Confession time.* "I saw you at the Cave."

John's head whirled right. "What? When?"

"The same night I had a meltdown at your place."

John leaned his head back and considered. "That was the first night I went there since the shooting."

"You seemed very popular."

He snorted. "I'm not a slut, if that's what you're insinuating."

"No." He ruffled John's already ruffled hair. "I mean you were like a puppy everyone wanted to pet and pass around."

"Why didn't you come up and say hello?"

He procrastinated with his bagel. "I'm not out. Not really. I've never even kissed a guy in public, not outside of dark alleys, at least. And certainly not since what happened in Charleston."

"Ominous." He leaned his head against Isaac's shoulder and chewed. Isaac was surprised how nonsexual it felt.

"I didn't leave my job at Broad College. I was sort of forced out."

"Not for being gay."

"Not in so many words," Isaac whispered.

John lifted his head, and his face assumed the same murderous expression it had during his speech the day before. "What? They can't fucking do that."

"It was suggested I should go due to the scandal of my divorce and the very loud outcries of my wife, also a professor at Broad."

"You should sue them!"

He sounded just like Simon.

"It didn't matter," Isaac said. "I needed to leave. I wanted to leave. I destroyed Elizabeth and broke my parents' hearts."

"By being yourself?"

He wanted John to understand. "By lying. For over a decade."

John flopped back against the headboard, rattling the whole thing. "And you thought Hambden would be the same? That they'd ostracize you for being gay?"

"Not really." He clicked his tongue. "Don't get angry, but I didn't want to be the token gay professor."

John hummed. "Good. I've owned that racket for years."

"You've always been open about it?"

He shrugged. "It was always such a big part of who I was. I sold a story to *The New Yorker* when I was seventeen, and it was about the first time I got beat up for being gay. Luckily, I've really filled out since then."

Isaac laughed into his coffee, which was lukewarm and weak. "How old are you now?"

"Old enough."

"Yeah, me too." Despite having his own bagel, he stole a piece of John's, which earned him a glare. "Hambden isn't utopia, though. You said people have been fired for interoffice romances in the past?"

"The Brown-Lancaster Debacle."

Isaac felt his face melt into a "What?" shape.

"Sounds cooler if you give it a name," John explained. "They were English professors who started banging. They were stupid about it and got caught messing around in Dr. Lancaster's office. Abby walked right in and…" He turned his palms up. "Both of them lost their jobs. And I guess they ended up breaking up, so it was all a stupid waste. I hear he's a crackhead now."

Isaac pondered this and elbowed John. "He is not."

John snorted.

"It's strange. Everyone seems so accepting at Hambden. I would have expected the no-shenanigans rule to be more suggestion than career suicide."

John shrugged. "Nope. It's a thing." He sighed. "You know, this has been a very enlightening weekend, Dr. Twain."

"Indeed it has, Mr. Conlon."

"Just don't ever kiss me again."

"Fine. I won't. It was gross."

John smacked him in the chest. "Fucker."

The truth was it hadn't been gross at all.

Chapter Six

AFTER SPENDING ALL of Sunday night thinking about how John's mouth tasted, Isaac looked forward to the distraction of the school week. He needed to immediately stop obsessing over his coworker, and he promised himself he would—as soon as he got to work. So what if he still reeled at the memory of touching John's hair, of the feel of that impeccable jaw in the palm of his hand?

Arriving early to his office, Isaac placed his laptop on his desk and planned to check email. First, he grabbed a cup of coffee from the machine in Cleo's office. She smiled and waved when he entered, chatting on the phone to what sounded like a worried student. She used soothing, quiet tones and dancing hand gestures as if the student in distress could see her.

Once Isaac had his coffee, he turned to step back into his office, nodding to a few other faculty members in the hall. Then, he saw John walking swiftly toward him, a white flyer in hand and his cell phone pressed to his ear. He was always a pale guy, but that morning, he looked almost blue.

"I'm not mad at you," he said into the phone, shoving the flyer at Isaac. "Janelle, I really need you to call me back. Please."

Isaac looked at the flyer. Across the top, in boxy, black letters were the words, *"Being Frank."* Below the words was a picture of Chris Frank with *x*'s over his eyes.

Isaac skimmed over the submission information, but he didn't really see the words. He gaped at John as he hung up his cell phone. Cold dread pooled in Isaac's gut.

"Where did this come from?" Isaac asked.

"They're hanging all over campus."

"I never saw this."

John grabbed the flyer back. "Shit, neither did I, Isaac." He pressed his lips together. "Sorry. This is not your fault."

"Janelle did this?"

"Apparently. She's not answering her phone." As if to clarify, John pulled his phone from his pocket and stared at the black screen hopelessly.

Tommy arrived at a jog holding a copy of the dreaded flyer. He flung it between Isaac and John. "Did you see this? Are you insane?"

"Are you going to lower your fucking voice?" John hissed. They were quickly drawing the attention of all faculty in the vicinity—which was most of the English Department since the majority of professors stopped by their offices first thing in the morning. "I didn't know about the flyers. Janelle must have printed them."

Tommy appeared to shrink behind his glasses. "Meeks is gonna have your head, man."

As if conjured by a dark spell, her voice echoed down the hall, shouting John's name.

John closed his eyes.

Meeks rounded the corner in a blue business suit, her long, dark hair in a high ponytail. Isaac thought her makeup was too thick, like she hid a whole other person under all that paint. Of course she had a flyer in her hand, and as she stomped toward John, Isaac had the irrational reflex to jump in front of him.

"What the hell is this?" She waved the half-crumpled flyer in his face.

"Sonya, I didn't know about the flyer, okay? One of the students went rogue. I'll fix it."

"You'll *fix it?*"

Now, everyone in the hall stared, heads craned out of offices, whispering behind hands.

"I forbid you from doing this." She threw the flyer at his feet.

"From doing what?"

"You will not produce this literary magazine."

He shook his head. "The literary magazine is a brilliant idea. I'm not dropping it."

"*Being Frank*? Do you know what effect that title will have on the student body?"

"It's supposed to have an effect." John's hair flew around his face. "It's supposed to start a conversation. I understand the flyers are completely out of line, but we're doing this literary magazine."

"Says who?"

"Says me."

Meeks pointed a finger in his face. "You will not publish a magazine about the shooting. There is no reason to scare the students and remind them what happened here."

"But it *did fucking happen*, Sonya!"

Meeks went silent. In fact, the whole hallway seemed empty of oxygen. They could have been in space.

After a moment that felt like centuries, Meeks glanced around at all the staring faces. She leaned close to John, but Isaac heard her whisper, "Let's talk about this in my office."

"Let's talk about this here." His eyes scanned the area. "Does anyone remember Demi Snyder? Cute little redhead with freckles? Does anyone remember the sound she made when she got shot? I remember. I remember her calling for help. I remember her blood on my hands, the way it felt too damn cold." John picked up the flyer Meeks had crumpled and thrown at his feet. He uncurled the edges so everyone could see Chris Frank and held the flyer in the air. "Something really bad happened last year, and I don't know why we're pretending it didn't."

No one spoke, not even Meeks, who now had John's full attention. He spoke right in her face.

"Six people are dead, and whether we talk about them or not, they're still dead. Even Abby. Do you remember our friend, Sonya?"

Jaw clenched, she turned away from him, so he addressed the now crowded hall.

"This literary magazine is an open forum for students who want to talk about what happened. You all want to whitewash a shooting? Fine. Or we can give the kids voices, let them write about how they're feeling. Let them write about the people they miss. I miss Demi. I even miss Chris." He turned to Meeks. "Either give this magazine the go-ahead or fire me."

"Jesus, John." Her shrewd, dark eyes turned to the floor.

"The kids need this. The school needs this."

She sighed and tapped her fingers against her lips, probably now in desperate need of a cigarette.

"I agree with John," Isaac said, not only to keep John from getting fired but also to prove he agreed with everything John had just said.

Other professors nodded, and Meeks looked like she had one hell of a headache. "Make new flyers. And you will keep me updated on everything."

"Fine."

"Don't let this get out of control." She turned away and said, "Show's over," before disappearing down the hall.

Foreseeing mass chaos, Isaac took John's arm and dragged him into his office, closing the door once Tommy was inside. John fell into Isaac's guest chair and buried his hands in his hair before bending forward at the waist as though he might puke.

Tommy leaned against the door. "Dude, I can't believe you actually used to be friends with that wench. I think my balls are in my abdomen right now."

John chuckled from beneath his slouch.

"No, man, that was like a scene out of a movie."

"I feel sick," John confirmed.

Isaac knelt in front of him and tried the trick Tommy had used before. "Hey. Breathe."

John looked like he was having trouble.

Tommy put his hand on John's shoulder. "You did good."

His gaze shifted to Isaac, still kneeling in front of him. "You got my back on this?"

If it gave him a purpose, a cause? A plausible excuse to spend more time with John? "For sure. I am your assistant faculty advisor."

"We've got to think of a cooler title."

Tommy looked at his watch and tried to tuck his wrinkled shirt into equally wrinkled khakis. "Shit, I have to teach or something. Martinis tonight? Crocodile Lounge. Jazz and gin. I'm buying."

"Yes, please." John leaned heavily against the back of the chair.

"Isaac, you in?"

"I'll be there."

"This is a *day*," Tommy said with cheerleader enthusiasm before stepping back into the hall and closing the door behind him.

"What did I just do?" John muttered. "Did I just give an Al Pacino monologue out there?"

Isaac stood and leaned against his desk.

"This is going to be an uphill battle, isn't it?"

"Yep." Isaac crossed his boat shoes. "But we can do it."

John's face wasn't good at hiding emotion. Every thought he had played out in the differing shades of his eyes, an up or downturn of his mouth. Sometimes, even his forehead expressed full sentences. For instance, in that moment, Isaac could see he was worried, scared even. He looked up at Isaac, and Isaac hoped he wasn't as transparent.

AT CROCODILE LOUNGE, Cleo and John were excellent salsa partners. Isaac knew they'd taken lessons together, but they were also of similar heights. Then, there was the rhythm: impeccable, thanks to Cleo's knowledge of music and John's...well, Isaac wasn't sure where he'd learned rhythm. It certainly wasn't part of English curriculum. Maybe it was his love of classic rock, or maybe he'd watched his parents waltz happily around the kitchen of his childhood home.

Tommy stood at Isaac's side, both men drinking Manhattans as Janelle and Anthony hopped around the dance floor. Apparently, she and John had talked earlier about her snafu. All Tommy would say was that it had been "intense" but that they'd eventually gone around campus together removing flyers.

John spun Cleo, and she let out a bright "Woohoo!"

"Hey, how was Ohioana anyway?"

"Fine," Isaac said quickly. Maybe too quickly. Every time he stopped to think, he tasted John's tongue in his mouth.

"Didn't have to bodyguard anyone?"

"I broke a couple kneecaps."

Tommy smacked his shoulder. "My man."

When an older gent in a suit asked John if he could cut in, John bowed to Cleo and headed their way. "Where's my drink?"

"I don't know," Tommy said. "Where is your drink?"

John batted his eyelashes, and Tommy groaned before turning around and ordering John a Manhattan too. John leaned on the bar next to Isaac and watched the band—a four-piece number that played salsa, swing, and just about everything else.

"Things good with you and Janelle?"

John lifted one shoulder. "We've fought before, and we'll fight again. She likes anarchy. When Demi was alive, they were the queens of protest. They even went to a couple gay marches with me."

"But you're obviously her favorite teacher."

"That's the thing. I don't know if she thinks of me as her teacher. More like her friend."

Isaac smiled. "Probably because you look like a student."

John stared pointedly at the side of Isaac's head. "Well, at least I don't have any gray hair."

Isaac blinked. "I do *not*."

He chortled and accepted a drink from Tommy. "Do you dance, Isaac?"

"No. Well, Southern men can waltz, I guess. I had to learn how for all the rich girl cotillions growing up."

Tommy reached behind his glasses and itched his eye. "Jesus, I can just see you in an oversized tuxedo and pastel cummerbund." He yawned and gestured to his drink. "This is it for me, guys. I'm not sure if I'm more emotionally or physically exhausted."

"*You're* emotionally exhausted?" John smacked his arm. "You're not the one who gave an impromptu screaming speech this morning."

"I'm sympathetically exhausted," Tommy said.

When a slow swing song began, Cleo motioned for John, who went to her side immediately. He spun her before pulling her back into his arms, and they floated across the floor like Fred and Ginger. Isaac watched John's hands—his long, thin fingers. He laughed and talked to Cleo as they moved, flash of white teeth, tip of a pink tongue. Cleo pushed hair behind his ear, and they danced cheek to cheek. So what if Isaac was jealous.

Tommy left, and the other "adults" didn't linger long after. Isaac, John, and Cleo stepped out into the crisp September night, while Janelle and Anthony remained dancing inside, along with a half dozen of their friends.

"Do you need me to walk you home?" John asked.

Cleo shrugged into a faux-fur coat. "I'll be fine. Thanks for the dance, as always, and thanks for today. It was..." She blinked and looked up at the stars. "I have no words."

"That's unlikely."

She quirked an eyebrow at them both. "Night!"

John and Isaac walked in the same direction, toward both their places. So convenient that Isaac's stairwell was right next to Crocodile Lounge. After taking a quick glance up and down Union Street, he opened the door and dragged John inside.

Behind the closed door, he pressed John against the wall and leaned in for a kiss, but John turned his head. "Isaac."

"Mm?" He rubbed his nose across John's cheek.

"I thought you said kissing me was the worst."

"I was wrong. *Not* kissing you is the worst."

John's lips parted when Isaac pressed their noses together, but he soon put his hand on Isaac's chest and pushed. "We can't."

Isaac pushed back and took hold of John's hips. "I can't stop thinking about you." Whatever *this* was, whatever they had together, Isaac wanted more—and not just because he was lonely or horny. He wanted specifically John, in the stairwell, over a desk, anywhere really.

He must have been doing something right, because John's breath caught in his throat, and his eyes closed. "You have to stop thinking about me. We can't..." He blinked and gave Isaac a soft shove. "Isaac?"

He stopped kneading John's hips but kept their foreheads pressed together as he took a long, slow breath. "You're right. Sorry."

Instead of pushing again, John put his hands on Isaac's face. "Behave."

"You smell good."

"Of course I smell good. I smell like Knob Creek."

"No, it's just you." Isaac stood up straight and leaned against the wall opposite. "I didn't think you'd be a problem for me."

John grinned. "Surprise! Now, go upstairs and go to bed. No running tonight. We have important literary magazine business tomorrow." He adjusted the lapel on Isaac's coat. "And no more kissing. Even if we maybe, sort of, totally want to."

He touched John's hand. "Fine."

"Good night," John said.

"Night."

John waved and opened the door to the street. His dark hair glowed in the glare of a nearby streetlight before he disappeared behind the swinging door. Isaac leaned his head forward and thumped it back into the wall. Deny it all he wanted, but Isaac longed to chase after him.

THE REVELATION OF *Being Frank* spread, thanks to Janelle's impromptu—and ill-advised—flyer campaign. While Isaac half expected protests outside their meeting that night, instead, more students arrived to volunteer. John rushed around chatting everyone up like the host of some grand soiree. He separated the students into groups based on skills and interests, so a couple of kids worked on the official flyer design, the type-A folks put together their deadline schedule, and the hard-core writers built criteria sheets every submission would be judged by. Janelle sat to the side observing, mingling here and there. Despite her ridiculous T-shirt that read "Brunettes Make Better Psychos," she seemed older than her classmates. Isaac wondered if the shooting had anything to do with it.

Type A himself, Isaac worked with the scheduling kids, although John checked in every once in a while. He would walk by, smile, and maybe squeeze Isaac's shoulder. Once, Isaac caught Janelle staring at them. What did she see?

Isaac didn't have to wonder long. After the meeting was adjourned, Janelle handed him a folded piece of paper and walked away, black hair bouncing behind her. He unfolded it.

John has a crush on you.

He refolded it and tried not to grin like a goose.

Isaac wrestled with his own resolve once he got home. The apartment, as always, was empty and awful. He turned on some James Taylor, but that didn't help, because it only reminded him of John singing on the way to the Ohioana.

"Screw it."

He plopped down on the couch and pulled out his phone and the note from Janelle. He snapped a photo and sent it to John with a quick message: *Note from Janelle. Is it true?*

It took a couple minutes, but John eventually responded: *No. You have too many muscles, and you make me feel safe. It's disgusting.*

Of course, Isaac had expected a joke, but the "safe" comment?

"Keep it light," Isaac muttered. He typed: *Good. Your hair is too silky, and I've never once thought about your mouth in the shower.*

He was rewarded with three laughing emojis.

Isaac was prepared for that to be the end of it, but his phone soon pinged with another text from John: *NFL Thursday night special. Party at my place 7 PM. No flirting or Tommy will beat you up.*

Isaac texted quickly: *I'm afraid flirting is now my biological response to you.*

Go take a shower.

If only that would be enough. He wanted John there on the couch, preferably on his lap. It was only nine o'clock. Isaac could go to the Cave and pick someone up—but what would that achieve? A release, for certain, but he already knew he'd be picturing John the whole time. He had some very choice images to build on, thanks to their time at the hotel in Columbus. Plus, there had been that bit of hair pulling at the Cave with that Adam guy. Did John like having his hair pulled? What else did John like?

A text: *Jesus, did I just break you?*

Isaac almost dropped his phone.

HE DIDN'T KNOW anyone but John and Tommy at the NFL party, but he thought he recognized a few of the other guests from that night at the Cave. Thankfully, Adam wasn't there. No matter the bartender said there was nothing going on between them, Isaac couldn't stand the idea of another guy kissing John—not that he had a bit of license to be jealous, no. He kept trying to get himself in check, and it would work for a couple hours, until he saw John again. Even being within a ten-foot radius was a distraction, and every time they were together, John looked at him—a lot. All John's stories were for Isaac now. Out at lunch that afternoon, he worried Tommy was beginning to feel like a third wheel.

John hurried into the kitchen where Isaac hid. "Why aren't you eating?"

Isaac glanced toward the impressive appetizer spread on the large island. "I will later." He lifted his glass of wine. "Liquid diet for now." He hoped the alcohol would calm the way his heart pounded whenever John was around.

From where he stood, he could see all of John's kitchen and living room and out onto the back porch where guys smoked. The open layout made the small house seem huge.

"Scoot." John hip checked Isaac out of the way so he could get to the fridge.

"I thought you liked *college* football."

"I do." He pulled out a bottle of bleu cheese dressing, presumably for the hot wings. The sauce scent burned Isaac's nostrils from five feet away. "I like all football, but I prefer college football because the University of Wisconsin is everything."

"Do you suppose Hambden ever feels slighted by your undergrad fixation?"

John blinked his big eyes up at him. In a thin black sweater that was a little too long in the sleeves, he might as well have written "Cuddle Me" across his forehead. "Isaac, they're not even in the same division."

"My mistake," Isaac muttered.

Tommy, decked out in Ohio State garb, even though Ohio State wasn't playing, shouted, "Kickoff" from the living room, and John hurried to his side, slinging an arm around Tommy's shoulders. They toasted with bottles of beer as the football on screen flipped and spun into the far-off New England air.

It wasn't that Isaac didn't like football. He just didn't care. He understood it could be a nice escape, but he'd always preferred escaping into books—especially now that he'd found award-winning author John Conlon. He was on his third book by then.

Watching John watch football was like watching a prizefight. He jumped on furniture and shouted and gave high fives. Tommy was no better, although he was less enthusiasm, more wrath. They acted as a counterbalance—good cop, bad cop—their shenanigans more entertaining than the game itself.

When Isaac's phone vibrated in his pocket, he should have known not to look. He'd grown so accustomed to ignoring it, but now, John texted him pretty often—stupid, silly things about classroom glitches, the crappy Ohio weather, and even one picture of John with bed head. But John was in the room, so he wasn't texting.

No, Simon texted—something simple, honest, and horrible: *You can't hide forever.*

Isaac closed his eyes and slumped against the nearest wall. He wondered how much time he had before Simon showed up in Lothos, and what the hell would he do then? Strangely, his thoughts shifted to John. What would John think if he knew about Simon? There certainly would be no more impromptu kisses. John might not even want to speak to Isaac anymore. He gulped down dread at the thought. John was already a friendly fixture—or fixation. Either way, Isaac had never felt so comfortable with someone before, and in his limited relationship experience, he assumed that was something worth holding onto.

A loud, collective moan from the living room interrupted his inner turmoil as a news announcement spoiled the night, but silence ruled when the headline flashed across the screen.

At least 120 dead in Barcelona attacks.

"What the fuck," Tommy muttered.

Isaac watched John, lips parted, eyes reflecting light from the TV.

The newscaster spoke in a clipped, British accent, but Isaac didn't hear all of it, just fragments. "We still don't have all the details...two explosions...team of gunmen... hundreds still trapped..."

At the sound of gunfire from some tourist's cell phone video, John covered his ears and curled his shoulders forward. He whimpered and audibly sucked air into his lungs. Isaac moved to protect, putting his hand on John's back, while Tommy practically shoved John into his arms. "Get him out of here," he said.

Before Isaac could move John anywhere, John hurried down the darkened hall toward the bathroom, Isaac right on his heels. John barely made it to the toilet before throwing up. He fell to his knees, and Isaac tried to keep his hair out of the way. As John choked, Isaac handed him a towel.

"I'm sorry," John muttered. "I get episodes. Sorry."

"Don't apologize, John."

He wiped his face, still gasping for breath. "Could you get me, uh, in the medicine cabinet, there's Klonopin?"

"Yeah." Isaac hurried over and read the labels on several orange bottles before finding the right one. "How many?"

"Just one." He sat back on his heels on the black tile floor.

Isaac joined him, handing him a small, pink pill that John swallowed without water.

"We should get back out there." He moved to stand, but Isaac pulled him back to sitting.

"Let's give it a minute." Isaac wasn't even thinking about Spain. All he could see was the man in front of him, trying desperately to hide the trembling of his hands.

John crawled past Isaac and reached under the sink for mouthwash. He swished and spit into the toilet before flushing. "God, this is embarrassing. You must think I'm a disaster."

Isaac put his hand on John's shoulder and squeezed. "No, I don't."

He coughed into his sleeve. "Who the fuck shoots up a cool place like Barcelona?"

Isaac scooted closer, their knees touching. "I assume you've been there?"

"I spent a couple summers in France with my mom's family when I was a kid. We'd hit up Spain sometimes."

"Your French is very sexy."

"Isaac, you just watched me vomit. I'm pretty sure my mystique is gone."

Someone knocked on the door, followed by Tommy's voice: "John?"

"Come in."

He stuck his head inside. "Need anything?"

"I'll come back out." He reached his hand up, and Tommy pulled him to standing.

They hugged—a tight, manly squeeze—but Tommy hesitated before letting John through. "The news is just getting worse. There are hostages in some theater. Lots of them."

John closed his eyes, and Isaac felt dizzy. *What possessed a person to kill innocent bystanders? What kind of blind hatred did it require to spray bullets into a crowd?*

"I think everyone's leaving. You know, loved ones and stuff. You two want to hit Joe's Pub or something?"

"I don't want to leave the house right now," John said.

Tommy winced. "Right. Duh."

"There's no 'duh,' okay?" John growled but quickly covered his face and spoke through spread fingers. "Sorry. Why don't you just go to Joe's and drink for me?"

"Who's going to help clean?"

Isaac stepped past them and into the hall. "I'll stay."

John started, "Isaac, you don't—"

He said, "It's no big deal," and headed for the kitchen. He needed to keep his hands busy and hopefully his mind too.

He attacked the dishes in the sink, partygoers still watching CNN. They'd switched stations, the game forgotten. Isaac didn't listen much. He focused on the task at hand, which eventually involved searching John's cupboards for Tupperware and putting leftovers in the fridge. By the time Isaac actually noticed his surroundings, he was alone with John, and the TV was black. They moved around and past each other, finishing the last of the dishes, putting things away.

John initiated first contact. He wrapped his hand around Isaac's wrist and pulled him close. He pressed his face against Isaac's chest, so Isaac put his hand in John's hair and held on. John eventually lifted up on his toes to kiss him, and whatever simmered between them rolled to a boil. As soon as Isaac tasted John's mouth again, he groaned, consequences be damned. He trapped John against the counter, boxing him in with arms on either side. Hands everywhere—petting, touching, pulling at clothes—John whispered, "Need you."

Isaac lifted him onto the counter and stepped between his parted legs. He slipped his hands up the back of John's sweater and kissed him hard. He sucked kisses down the side of John's neck until his head leaned back. He licked the soft skin, the place where Chris Frank once pressed a gun.

With ease, he lifted John from the countertop and carried him, legs around Isaac's waist, to the bedroom. He kicked open the door. Dim light from the kitchen trickled down the hallway and poured in a pie-slice shape onto the ruffled, unmade bed. Isaac took hold of John's hips and threw him down the center of a black-and-white down comforter. On the bed, John backed up on his elbows and feet, kicking blankets away as Isaac tumbled on top of him. Isaac vaguely heard John exhale a *whoosh* of air at the sudden arrival—just as Isaac used his knees to press John's thighs apart. He shoved that all-too-tempting sweater from earlier up John's arching torso, revealing two small nipples that Isaac leaned down and bit.

John made a sound like he'd been punched, back arching more, mouth wide in what Isaac could discern in the dark. Isaac knew what to do, had moves memorized from so many harried trysts with strange men in even stranger places. He leaned back and tugged at the button of John's jeans, eyes watching his own hands move. Button free, he tugged at the zipper and was about to tear those skinny jeans right off when pale, delicate hands wrapped around his.

"Isaac?"

He closed his eyes and shook his head. When he opened them again, he recognized John beneath him, not some nameless stranger in a bar. He drew his hands away and leaned back on his heels as John stretched to reach the lamp on the side table. A click and the room glowed soft gold. Isaac saw the scattered pile of books by the lamp, the empty water glass and tube of lip balm. Then, he noticed John, shaggy dark hair askew, half in his eyes, and lips wet and parted. The sweater still rested up under his armpits, revealing those tiny, pink nipples and broad, hairless chest. Down his prominent ribs, his hips curved in at the sides in a skinny V. Nothing but a few sparse dark hairs decorated his lower belly, disappearing into black underwear beneath the open fly of his jeans.

Isaac's breath shook.

"Isaac?" John scooted closer, thighs still on either side of Isaac's. He sat up, and Isaac slumped down. "Hey, where are you right now?" He put his hand to Isaac's face, and Isaac didn't hesitate to kiss his palm.

"You're so small," he said.

John smiled, fingers tracing Isaac's face. "I'm not *that* small."

"Compared to the men I usually take to bed."

John kissed his collarbone. Words like a warm breeze caressed his skin. "I'm not them."

John was nothing like all those secretive one-night stands. He wasn't even like imposing Simon—Simon, who Isaac had loved and who liked to play rough because that was what big, strong men did. John was John, an emotionally busted creative writing teacher whose hands felt as breakable as bird wings and who probably bruised at the lightest touch. John was his coworker, his friend.

No matter how much Isaac had previously thought he wanted this, warring emotions of guilt and anxiety, worship and need, blurred his brain. He shook his head. "Shit, we shouldn't—"

John lurched up into his arms, mouth on Isaac's. He was a persistent kisser, licking and nibbling while filling the bedroom with delicious, breathy moans. He broke away just long enough to pull Isaac's shirt over his head. "I want you to fuck me," he whispered.

"Jesus, your voice..." Isaac melted on top of John, but only after pulling his black sweater the rest of the way off his slight frame. With John's legs wrapped around him, it was impossible for Isaac to miss how much John *wanted.* Isaac rolled his hips in response and watched in awe as

John's mouth dropped open, head thrown back. The center of his chest already glistened with sweat. "You're so goddamn beautiful."

By the time John reached for the lube in his bedside table, they were both halfway out of their pants, rutting like teenagers. As John dug around for condoms, Isaac removed his own jeans before tugging on John's—and tugging John halfway down the bed in the process. John laughed, a high-pitched musical sound, so foreign to Isaac in sexual situations. Sex had always felt like a task to be accomplished, something to finish. And yet, here was John, laughing as Isaac wrestled to get his feet out of his skinny jeans.

Once successful at his task, Isaac crawled up the bed, rubbing every inch of his naked skin against John's but not before sucking his hip bones and pressing his nose against the center of John's chest. He balanced on one elbow while his other hand cupped John's jaw, thumb running across his pink bottom lip.

John held up the bottle of lube. "Do you want to? Or do you want to watch me?"

Isaac snatched the bottle. "Are you kidding?" He added a couple of drops to his fingers before moving slowly to reach between John's parted legs, but John halted his progress, hands digging into Isaac's shoulders.

"Be gentle at first?"

The slight trepidation in those big, green eyes made Isaac want to hide. He whispered, "I'm sorry I was rough earlier."

"Rough is fine. You just have to work up to it." He wrapped his arms around Isaac's neck. "Although you can pull my hair anytime."

"Oh, yeah?"

John nodded and licked along the seam of Isaac's lips until Isaac sucked his eager tongue into his mouth.

When Isaac pressed his first finger all the way inside, he suspected there was no way they would ever be able to have sex. "You're so tight."

Eyes squeezed shut, John muttered, "But very accommodating. Just go slow."

Later, three fingers in, Isaac further suspected he would never last long enough to actually fuck the writhing, pleading man beneath him. John chewed his lips so much, Isaac worried they might bleed. If Isaac's hand lingered too long, caressing the lean muscle of John's chest, John would grab Isaac's hand and put it back in his hair until Isaac did as bid: grabbed a fistful and pulled.

John suddenly clutched to his biceps. "Please. Please, please, please." Hazy eyes blinked up at Isaac; he would have given John anything he asked for in that moment.

Despite John's begging, Isaac had to lean back to put on the condom. Before pushing into John's wanting body, Isaac had the fleeting thought: *This is a terrible idea.* And not because of the nonfraternization policy or Simon or John's floundering mental health. It was terrible because Isaac was already half gone on the man below him, lured in by his charisma like everyone else in town. More than that, he wanted to shield and protect. Isaac had never been good at either of those things, but he was good at fucking.

He pressed into John's body slowly until John winced and said, "Stop, just for a second." Isaac waited and leaned down to press kisses all over John's face. Then, a moment later: "Okay."

Isaac tilted his hips forward. John's heels dug into the backs of his thighs as they both moaned.

"I knew you would feel good," John said. He kissed Isaac's forehead and ran his hands through Isaac's hair while Isaac felt the much-hated, long-despised burn of salt behind his eyes. Instead of crying over John's unexpected tenderness, he pulled his hips back and thrust forward. John yelled, "Oh, fuck," but Isaac didn't stop. He kept going rough and fast until John's hands lifted above him to keep them both from ramming into the headboard.

John's voice trembled with the rhythm of Isaac's thrusts. "Fuck, there's going to be nothing left of me."

Isaac pulled out and easily flipped John onto his stomach. He thrust back into him. Both John's hands clenched to the sheets below him. His spine arched as he pressed onto all fours, continuing to welcome Isaac's body into his by way of sibilant consonants and weak whispers of Isaac's name. John eventually melted onto his elbows, but Isaac held his hips in the air, fingers pressing into flesh and bone. He thought about John's pale skin, how it would probably bruise, but was beyond the point of caring. He never wanted to hurt John, but the way John begged for "harder" and "more" only spurred Isaac on.

John finished first, face twisted to the side so Isaac could just make out the wrinkled profile of his face, mouth in the shape of an O. Isaac kept going, never wanting to stop. If only his whole world could be this beautiful creature beneath him, the one who now allowed Isaac to pull out again and flip him onto his back.

Isaac lifted John's knees over his shoulders and continued the amazing fuck he never wanted to end. John trembled and twitched and begged "please" some more, although this time, he begged for relief from Isaac's need to stretch things out—his need to pound the heartbreak out of John and into the ether where it could swallow some cruel killer or murdering thief instead of this Hambden hero.

As if hearing his thoughts, John took hold of Isaac's face. "It's okay. Come for me?"

Isaac pressed his forehead against John's collarbone, finishing with a groan that sounded like a sob.

Chapter Seven

IN THE MORNING, Isaac knew straightaway he wasn't in his own bed. His sheets weren't this soft. His bed sagged in the middle, and he never had this much legroom. Plus, there wasn't usually a warm body curled against his side, breathing softly. Eyes popped open, he found a sleeping— and bare-shouldered—John next to him, knees curled against his hip. Isaac didn't move.

Based on the dim light coming through the gauzy curtains of John's bedroom, it couldn't be much past seven. Last night, they'd...

He squeezed his eyes shut as images flashed like photos through his mind. They'd had sex. And someone had shot up Barcelona. And Simon had texted.

How had he forgotten that detail? Simon hadn't given up. He was still looking for him, and yet, here Isaac was having the best sex of his life.

Was it the panic of waking next to John that made him slide out of bed or the knowledge that Simon might show up in Lothos? He couldn't find out about John. John couldn't become a target, not again.

Isaac had thought it the night before, and he thought it again. *A terrible idea.*

On the bed, the man Isaac wanted to protect shifted, moaned, but didn't wake. Isaac scooped up his clothes and tiptoed into the hall. He dressed quickly, quietly, and left the house without making a sound.

Back in his own apartment, he turned the shower to scald and scraped his skin clean. He brushed his teeth twice and hurried to campus, where he had an early composition class.

On the third floor of Ellis Hall, Isaac tried not to be the worst teacher in the history of the department. He tried to lecture. He tried to listen; he really did, but his mind would not engage. His mind was stuck somewhere in the vicinity of midnight the night before, then two, three thirty.

John bit his bottom lip when close to orgasm. Sweat tended to pool between his pecs, and he wasn't hairless everywhere. His surprisingly deep voice cracked when he begged, and a passion for hair pulling was no longer theoretical but a proven fact. Isaac should not have known all those things. He also should not have been thinking about them in the middle of a discussion on thesis statements.

And Barcelona. Kids wanted to talk about Barcelona. The media wasn't reporting the full death toll yet, but it was over two hundred. No terrorist group had stepped forward, but everything had been organized, orchestrated, choreographed. The world felt cloaked in darkness.

When ten rolled around, Isaac rested his hands on the podium as students filed out, chatting amongst themselves. He looked up when one lingered, but it wasn't a student; it was John.

AT DONKEY, THEY sat on opposite sides of the purple couch, and John stared at the coffee cup in his hands. He cleared his throat and glanced around. "Was I really that awful? Because I've sure as fuck never had complaints before."

Isaac *tsked* and shook his head. "Jesus, John, you're the sexiest thing I've ever slept with. I couldn't focus in class at all."

John kept his voice low, but the anger was palpable. "Then, why did you leave?"

"I panicked."

"Grow up. It happened. We happened. Christ, you *wanted* it to happen. You think I don't notice the way you've been looking at me?"

Isaac gazed out toward the big glass windows that led to the street because every time he looked at John, he wanted to kiss him. Back in the classroom, he'd been ruffled, his eyes puffy like he hadn't gotten enough sleep. Isaac knew he hadn't. Even his lips were a different shade—darker, broadcasting to the world: "Isaac Twain sucked my lips last night."

John shifted an inch closer. "Can we talk about this like adults?"

Isaac forced himself to make eye contact. "It was amazing, and we shouldn't have done it."

"I'm aware," John said quietly. "It's my fault really. I was upset."

Masking his disappointment, Isaac forced himself to study John's expression. "Is that the only reason you did it?"

He frowned, eyes wrinkled at the edges. "What? No. I like you, Isaac. I always have."

"I like you, too, but for the sake of our jobs, we can't do this." He didn't bring up Simon. If he could break things off using another excuse, damn it, he would.

John was silent for a while, taking a few careful sips of hot coffee. He eventually ran his hand over his thigh like maybe his palms were sweating. "Why do you have angry sex?"

Isaac leaned forward. "Christ, did I hurt you?"

He had the gall to roll his eyes, but it might have been a defense mechanism. "You would have known if you'd been hurting me, okay? You just don't seem angry in life, so I don't know why it shows up in bed."

"No one's ever told me that before." No one had said it directly, but Isaac should have guessed. He was dominant in bed with other men because it was the only place in life where he felt in control.

"Maybe no one's told you because you disappear in the morning?"

"Ouch." He spent a few seconds picking at a perfectly fine fingernail. "I'm sorry I left." He reached out and touched one of John's tangled curls. "Looks like the knot goblin came back."

"Lucky your hair's so short, or he would have come for you too."

"So this thing between us is out of our systems now. We can just move on like nothing happened."

John tapped the mug in his hand. "There are plenty of tall, buff, blond guys in the sea. Or choose your metaphor. Let's just not be awkward, okay?"

Isaac held out his hand. "Friends?"

"Friends." John took it, and touching him was the worst idea Isaac had had in months.

They did their best to look like they weren't rushing, but after they downed their coffees, they might as well have been chased up Union Street. As soon as they banged through the door of Isaac's stairwell, they were on each other, coffee-flavored tongues mingling as they stumbled up steps. Isaac actually tripped and fell right on his hip. He winced, while John tried to hide his laugh.

"Oh, God, are you okay?"

Isaac stood and picked him up, wrapping John's legs around his waist. He pinned his thin wrists above his head and sucked the side of his neck. "I'd like to tie you up sometime."

John hit his head against the wall. "Never happening. I feel helpless enough with you around."

"When's your next class?"

John pulled him closer with his legs. "We have time."

"I can work with that," Isaac said.

John draped his arms around his shoulders and allowed himself to be carried into the crappy apartment, brighter because he was there.

LACKING IN SUPPLIES, Isaac enjoyed the full experience of *tasting* a morning John Conlon, his skin scent a mix of herbal body wash and witch hazel. On Isaac's tongue, John was sweet and salty all at once. Having never had an addictive personality before, Isaac worried now. He worried he would need the taste of John every day.

Sticky and sprawled together under cheap sheets, John stretched out across Isaac's chest and hummed. Isaac kissed his forehead and brushed his hair with his fingers.

"Can't believe we just messed around in a twin-sized bed."

John leaned up on his elbow. "I can't believe you didn't accidentally break my face against the bedframe last night."

"Sorry." He bumped his fingers down the nubs of John's spine. "Don't take this the wrong way, but I never had sex with a man your size before."

John's forehead wrinkled.

Isaac reached up to rub the wrinkles away. "I don't think *delicate* is the right word, but..."

"Oh." John smiled. "You mean a pretty little twink."

He groaned. "I always think that phrase has negative connotations."

John sucked Isaac's thumb into his mouth and let it go with a *pop*. "Nah. I know I sort of look like a girl. Made me super popular with the closeted jocks in college." He winked.

"What?" Isaac lifted his head and folded his pillow so he could better see John's face.

"You really want story time right now?"

"I'm sorry we didn't get to have it this morning," Isaac said.

"After that last blow job, I forgive you."

Isaac squeezed his side, and John twitched.

"No tickling."

He pulled John back down to rest on top of him and closed his eyes. "Tell me about these closeted jocks. I want a visual."

"I lived with five other guys at Wisconsin. Our house was known as the V, the place where people could swipe their V-cards."

"V-cards?"

"Lose their virginity."

Isaac cussed.

John's hand ran up and down Isaac's chest. "We'd have all these parties, huge keggers and shit. Of course, the gay guys would always go right for me, but I remember there was this football player. I had such a crush on him. Big, built dude. But he was straight, supposedly. One night, he followed me into the bathroom, and we just started kissing."

"I think I'm getting hard again."

John's laughter was a breeze across his nipple. "He asked me to go down on him, so I did. We never talked about it after. We'd see each other on campus, and he'd just walk right by."

Isaac would have been a nervous wreck, just waiting for a forced shove from the metaphorical closet. "How did he know you wouldn't say anything?"

"What was there to say? It wasn't my job to out him. And he was nice to me. Not everybody was."

Something in that tone… Isaac lifted his head. "What do you mean?"

"I think some guys in college hated that they were attracted to me. Sometimes, I'd get in fights. Other times, the sex might hurt a little."

Isaac lifted his head higher.

"Stop looking at me like that. I wasn't assaulted."

"Are you sure? I know men don't often come forward."

Patented John eye roll. "Please. The weirdest thing about the rough guys? They were the ones who wanted to cuddle after. They'd count my ribs or taste my skin like I was something precious when, in reality, they were just saying goodbye."

"You are such a writer."

He laughed and rested his chin in the center of Isaac's chest. "I only had one repeat offender at Wisconsin: Ben. He was openly gay too. We were off and on for three years. Maybe more friends than lovers, but we did have a really good time."

"I'll bet."

"You said you were with a guy in school?"

"Patrick," Isaac said. "Probably the worst sex of my life."

"First time usually is."

He absentmindedly curled pieces of John's hair around his fingers. "We didn't know what we were doing. We had zero business having intercourse, and we never talked about it afterward. The strangest part? Nothing changed. This earth-shattering thing had happened to me, and Patrick never acknowledged it. It was my ruination, I guess, because that experience solidified my attraction toward men but didn't allow me the freedom of admitting it."

"You can admit it now."

He shook his head. "No, I can't. No one can find out about us."

"Oh. Right. Fuck." John hid his face near Isaac's armpit. "I've never had a covert love affair before."

Isaac almost said, "I have" but shivered instead.

Isaac escaped soon after for his second shower of the day, turning the water to full heat. He almost shouted at the pain but gritted his teeth and scrubbed. He slipped a little when John stepped in behind him and screamed, "Jesus Christ, your skin's going to melt off." John turned on the cold water until the shower rinsed their sweat-soaked bodies at a normal temperature.

They both had work, classes to teach and papers to grade. John gave him a lingering kiss on his way out.

Isaac was quick to ask, "Are you okay walking alone?"

John tilted his head and must have understood the silent insinuation: *You had a meltdown last night after watching the news and didn't want to leave your house.* "I'm fine. I'm heavily medicated today."

Isaac waited ten minutes to make his own exit but watched the streets like a paranoid criminal in a bad TV thriller.

Chapter Eight

STANDING IN JOHN'S living room, Isaac watched the news wrap-up for the day. All the Barcelona shooters had been killed, but that didn't seem to help much. After all, Chris Frank was dead, too, but Hambden University was still a haunted place. Who knew when Barcelona would recover? He'd overheard John talking to his mom earlier—in French, so he didn't understand any of it. The tone had been less than cheerful. Now, a newscaster discussed the victims as food sizzled in the kitchen.

"Turn that shit off," John said. "You're the worst dinner guest ever."

"Sorry. Sorry."

"Ambulance chaser."

Isaac pushed a button, and the screen went black. "I'd rather chase you. Naked."

"Nobody looks good running naked, Isaac."

Music played from the kitchen—a mix on John's computer of classic rock and some modern folk. He tended to play music often when in the midst of mindless tasks. Isaac knew he even had Amazon Echo in his bathroom for when he showered.

It had been ages since a guy had offered to cook dinner for Isaac, but it wasn't as though he and John could be seen in public on dates. Not that he minded. John's house was already starting to feel like home. He walked into the kitchen and noticed the rich smell of butter and garlic. John stood at the stove in a tight, striped sweater that was testing the hell out of Isaac's resolve. He fed his alarming addiction to John's skin by pressing his front to John's back and wrapping his arms around his waist.

"That smells amazing."

"Mm." John tossed a teaspoon of something green into the skillet.

"Wait, are you domestic?" He tugged John closer. "You can dance. You keep a clean house. I've actually seen you hand-wash a sweater. *And* you can cook?" He kissed the side of his neck. "You're going to make someone a wonderful wife someday."

He wrestled out of Isaac's grip. "Cut it out. Pour the wine, you ass."

"I think teasing you is my new favorite hobby."

"Great."

Isaac did as instructed, never once taking his eyes off the one thing that currently made him happy—well, John and the literary magazine. Weeks since its inception, submissions had opened only the day before, and nobody knew what to expect, but Isaac still felt such a relief at being part of something—something good.

"Come here and fill your own plate," John said. "I don't like deciding people's meat-to-potato ratio."

With one hand on John's hip, he studied the stovetop spread. "What are we eating exactly? And don't give me French names for things. If I'm eating pig intestines, I want to know."

"Don't be ridiculous. We only eat pig intestines at Christmas. Seared and baked pork tenderloin with peppercorns, sage, and rosemary. *Pommes duchesse,* which are just specialty potatoes, you idiot, and steamed green beans."

Isaac kissed him just as they heard the front door open.

"John?"

"Fuck." John took a quick step back as Tommy barreled into the room—and stopped suddenly.

"Oh, shit, sorry." Hair in windblown spikes, he looked around the room. "Literary magazine business?"

"Yeah." John cleared his throat. "What's up? Did you just run up my hill?"

"I'll leave the running to Isaac, thank you." He helped himself to John's fridge as Isaac stepped to the clear opposite side of the island to put some space between himself and the man he couldn't stop touching. "I was at Joe's." He took a long gulp of beer, not even wasting the time to straighten his glasses. "Ran into Adam. Jesus, man, what possessed you to sleep with him?"

John's entire face wrinkled and relaxed, eyes to the ceiling.

"He kept asking if you were okay. I had to physically remove myself from the situation to get him to shut up."

Like vomit, the words couldn't be stopped. Isaac felt them coming up, up... "You slept with Adam?"

Time stopped.

"You know Adam?" Tommy asked.

John crossed his arms. "How do you know Adam?"

He had to backpedal, fast. "Oh, no, I must be thinking of someone else."

"Anyway." Tommy moved on, but John kept watching Isaac with squinted eyes. "Could you just call him and catch up? I'm not your secretary."

"Oh, as if I've never played wingman for you."

"This isn't wingman." Tommy pointed at himself. "This is a human walkie-talkie." He imitated a robot voice.

"John, I want to have a hundred of your babies. Over and out."

John shoved Tommy in the shoulder. "Jesus, get plates, you fuckers."

Well, apparently their romantic dinner date was over as Tommy did indeed fill a plate. The three men sat around the small table near the sliding porch door, the tiny white lights of Lothos in the distance. Tommy took a huge bite of meat with potatoes, followed by a gulp of beer, and groaned.

"Damn, John, if I were gay, I'd marry you."

"You did call yourself a lesbian once."

Tommy nodded, while Isaac tried not to make obscene noises while he chewed. Bless John Conlon's cooking.

"Didn't you have a date last night?"

Tommy grumbled, "She was a philosophy professor."

"I thought professors weren't allowed to date other professors," Isaac said.

"Only in the same department," Tommy replied. "Not that any of the women in the English Department are exactly beauty queens. But philosophy? I don't know what I was thinking. I know nothing about philosophy. As soon as she started talking Simone de Beauvoir's existential feminist blah-blah, I zoned out."

"You should find a kinesiology professor," Isaac said. "Mechanics of body movement and all that."

John smiled into his food, but Tommy's eyes lit up.

"Genius. This guy's a genius. Any Lothos locals caught your eye, Isaac?"

"Oh, I—"

"There's a tall drink of water over in administration," Tommy said between chews. "She wouldn't give me the time of day, but she might dig your whole rugged runner thing—although your chin looks soft as a baby's bottom lately. Give up on the five-o'clock shadow?"

He had, yes, because John's skin was sensitive. He shaved every morning now.

Tommy just kept talking. "I could introduce you two."

Isaac didn't even have to lie. "Tommy, I went through a divorce last year, so I'm kind of off women for a while. Thanks, though."

"Oh, man, I'm sorry. I had too much caffeine today. I promise not to play matchmaker." He dug back into his food. Isaac caught John trying not to laugh around a mouthful of green beans.

The three of them polished off dinner and cleaned the kitchen, after which Tommy finally left. "Guess I should let you two actually talk business," he said before flashing a peace sign and disappearing into the night.

JOHN'S DICK FIT perfectly into Isaac's mouth and down his throat, almost as if their bodies had been waiting, searching, and finally found their missing puzzle pieces. Isaac went down on John every chance he got; the addiction was less concern and more reality—however, John did not seem to mind. Slunk down in the couch, he bucked up into Isaac's mouth while cussing.

By the end, Isaac had to hold John's hips steady to keep him from arching off of it. John's hands clutched to the cushions above, head thrown back, as he bit his bottom lip. They'd been at it for a while by then, Isaac more than willing to delay dessert. He knew exactly what John liked, but he also knew the fun in waiting.

John put one hand in Isaac's hair. "I know you like teasing me, but please."

Isaac looked up and smiled but did ultimately lean forward so John could thrust right down his throat while Isaac moved his tongue in waves until John came in openmouthed silence.

"God, I love doing that to you." Isaac sat back on his knees and wiped his hand across his mouth.

"I've noticed. I thought we were going to watch a movie."

"We are, but I couldn't help myself. That sweater was driving me insane."

"This old thing?" John pulled up his jeans and buttoned them. "I realize you were probably trying to distract me with excellent head, but how do you know Adam?"

Isaac groaned and climbed onto the couch.

"Don't tell me you slept with him too? You guys would make zero sense in bed."

"No," he sighed. "I saw him at the Cave. With you. All over you. The bartender said you weren't a couple."

"We weren't. We aren't. We never have been." He ran a hand through his hair. "He's just a friend I ill-advisedly fucked."

"The same night I saw you there."

John touched his lips. "I'd just gotten back from Wisconsin, you know, and he was making all the right moves."

"Neck kissing and hair pulling."

John grimaced. "Does *everyone* know that shit about me?"

"I merely observed. Well, and tested the hypothesis. Many, many times."

He leaned his head against Isaac's shoulder. "Anyway, let's just say I hadn't gotten laid in a long time. And I'm not sleeping with him now. I'm sleeping with you. Sorry Tommy ruined our dinner."

"Dinner was amazing. You're amazing."

Eventually, they snuggled down into the couch—John's head on a pillow, his sock-clad feet in Isaac's lap. He gave John's arches a squeeze. "You have surprisingly large feet."

"The only way I keep my balance in the wind."

Isaac rubbed his feet and up the backs of his calves until, about twenty minutes into Spielberg's newest, John fell into the heavy limpness of sleep. Isaac made it about an hour before he turned off the TV, which roused John from slumber.

He leaned up on his elbows and stared around the room.

"Did you like the movie?" Isaac joked.

"Mm."

"You fell asleep five seconds in."

"It's your fault for sucking me off and then expecting me to pay attention."

"For that, I take full responsibility." Isaac ducked forward, pushed his shoulder into John's stomach, and lifted John up into the air.

John squealed in surprise as Isaac carried him toward the bedroom. "Wait. Lights!"

With John still folded over his shoulder, Isaac dutifully walked through the kitchen and living room until the house was dark. He headed for the bedroom, but John wasn't done with his orders.

"Bathroom! Drugs!"

"It's a good thing you're so light."

Still over Isaac's shoulder, John managed to open the medicine cabinet, swallow his pills, and even grab his mouth guard.

"Are you done?"

John imitated Isaac's voice as a high-pitched whine.

Finally, in the warmth of the bedroom, Isaac tossed John onto the cozy comforter and crawled on top of him. He kissed the base of his neck. "I like throwing you around. I could get used to dating someone your size."

John ran his fingertips over Isaac's cheeks. "Why don't you just get used to dating me?"

EVEN IN THE dark, Isaac recognized her shadow at the bottom of John's bed. Naked, Elizabeth crept in the moonlight. After he looked up and whispered her name, she stabbed her stomach once, twice, again and again until blood trickled down her legs. Then, blood rushed from between her thighs and pooled on the floor.

"Isaac."

How could one body bleed so much?

"Isaac."

Someone reached for him in the dark. Isaac gripped hard on sinew and skin until someone shouted his name.

He opened his eyes to find John's bedroom bright with lamplight.

"Isaac? It's me. Isaac? Can you let go, please?" John's voice sounded muddled at Isaac's side. It was the mouth guard he wore. He said he'd been grinding his teeth ever since the shooting.

Isaac searched the room for Elizabeth. When he didn't find her, he realized he held John's wrist in his hand—hard. "Shit." He let go, red finger marks evident. "Did I hurt you?"

John chuckled around the piece of plastic on his teeth. "A little."

"Ice. I'll get—" Isaac jumped out of bed and ran to the kitchen in search of some frozen corn or peas or something. When he got back to bed, John had removed the silly mouth guard. He opened and closed the fist of his left hand.

"I'm okay, really," he said when Isaac pressed a bag of mixed vegetables to his skin.

Isaac pushed John's hair from his forehead and kissed every inch of his face.

"Isaac. Hey. Stop. What just happened?"

"Nothing." He pressed his nose against John's and breathed in the sweat-sweet smell of his naked lover.

"Nothing? I thought you were going to punch me out."

"Just a nightmare," Isaac said. "Nothing."

"You want to tell me about it?"

"No." He held John's face in his hands and kissed both cheeks before helping John hold the frozen veggies to his wrist. "Keep that there. God, I hope I didn't give you bruises."

"Did you know I take pills for nightmares?"

Isaac nodded. "The ones you take before bed."

"Yeah. It's hell if I forget."

They leaned their heads together. "Are they always about the shooting?"

"No. Permutations of it maybe. It's always chaos. I can't see what's happening, but I know something bad is coming. My therapist says it's just anxiety."

Isaac shook his head and hazarded a glance below the bag of ice. John's wrist was still red, but at least the finger marks had gone away. "I never want to hurt you."

John smirked. "Well, it might not be intentional. You thought I was the monster in your dream."

"You're no monster."

He leaned his nose against Isaac's ear and whispered, "Sure, I am. We often look the sweetest."

Chapter Nine

THE EXCITEMENT WAS practically visible, floating like clouds of smoke near the buzzing fluorescent lights. All the literary magazine staff crowded around behind John's computer—John, who'd been sure to wear not only a long-sleeved shirt that day but a blazer, too, just in case he was tempted to roll up his sleeves. Yes, he had bruises in the shape of Isaac's fingers on his wrist. Yes, Isaac felt terrible, but John kept shrugging it off.

"I'm pale," John had said that morning. "People leave marks."

"What people?"

"Shit, Isaac, I had your thumbprint on my hip for two days after the first time we fucked."

Isaac had promised himself to be more careful.

Now, they had received their first email submission to *Being Frank*, and students jostled for position to read over John's shoulder. "Don't suck; don't suck," John said before clicking.

Anthony leaned closest to the screen as a dozen eyes skimmed. "It fucking sucks," he said.

John glared at him. "Anthony."

Isaac really tried not to look amused, but so it was in the world of creative writing: some was good, but most was bad. The only kid not immersed in pointing out everything wrong with their premiere submission was Janelle, who hovered by the darkened window in a

Spanish flag T-shirt. A cigarette would have looked perfectly at home in her hand. She stared down at College Green, so Isaac joined her.

"Don't you want to see the first submission?" he asked.

She shrugged and itched at the black bracelets on her arm. "Early days. We'll get more. Did John admit to his crush on you yet?"

"Why do you think he has a crush on me?"

"Because every time he talks, he looks around to make sure you're listening."

Isaac hadn't even noticed, but she was right. He hoped he didn't do the same. "We couldn't date anyway. It's against the rules."

"According to my parents' checkbook, I can't be a lesbian until I graduate, but I've done that just fine." She chewed a black-painted fingernail. "You seem cool, like, easy to talk to."

He leaned his shoulder against the wall by the window. "Most people just think I'm quiet."

"Maybe that's why you're easy to talk to," Janelle said. "You're not always lecturing like some of the other teachers."

"John doesn't lecture. Is that why you like him?"

She made a sound that was sort of a laugh but wasn't. "John's not a teacher. He's a writer."

"Can't he be both?"

She used her sleeve to rub at a thumbprint on the glass. "I like John because he doesn't bullshit. I heard about the way he stood up for this, for us. Guess I almost got him fired, huh?"

"Dr. Meeks wouldn't have gone through with it."

Janelle shook her head. "After what happened last year, he's the school's crown jewel. Higher-ups want to keep him around, but he's barely holding it together." Kohl liner made her eyes glow. "Haven't you noticed? I guess you didn't know him before, though. He was different. Before."

Isaac swore he felt a cold breeze. "Are you okay, Janelle?"

"About as okay as everyone else around here, Dr. Twain." She poked his arm. "Now, let's go see how much this submission sucks and make ourselves feel better about our own writing abilities."

She balanced on the edge of the desk near John and leaned forward, long, dark hair like a curtain covering her face. She scratched at her black bracelets, and Isaac concluded—quite easily really—that they hid scars.

JOHN'S BACKYARD, BRIGHT green when Isaac had first seen it in September, was now painted shades of orange and red—both the tree limbs above and fallen leaves below. The scent of wet earth wafted like perfume on the breeze. People filled a picnic table, as well as a few ramshackle tables that looked like they were probably campus castoffs. Cleo sat across from Isaac in an oversized sweater, black skull in the center, wielding a butcher knife—which would have been distressing if not for the huge pumpkin in front of her.

Isaac glanced over his shoulder at the click of a lighter and watched John pull smoke into his lungs before laughing with a few men whose names Isaac had already forgotten.

"I didn't know John smoked."

"It's a clove," Cleo said. "John and I split a pack once a year to celebrate Halloween."

John exhaled, and Isaac tore his gaze away. He'd never found smoking sexy until that second. "But you sing, Cleo. You shouldn't smoke."

"Once a year, Dr. Twain." She stabbed the top of her pumpkin and started sawing up, down, up, down.

"I haven't carved a pumpkin in years," Isaac muttered, his own kitchen knife in hand.

She paused. "Where have you been?"

"Unhappy." Before she could respond, Isaac plunged the knife in deep and immediately smelled pumpkin innards, despite John's fragrant clove smoke that now danced through the backyard.

The door into the house slid open, and Tommy's voice echoed through the yard. "Hey, asshole, get inside. Kickoff."

John whooped and dropped his clove into an empty beer bottle. Only four p.m., there were already several since John had apparently bought out the grocery store's supply of pumpkin beer and decided to share it with everyone—including Adam, who sat across the table and two seats down.

Adam was good-looking in that unfair sort of way, like John. They were both handsome but pretty and unlike anything Isaac had ever seen. That included Adam's hair—a thick, blond ponytail curled into a bun on the top of his head while the sides were shaved. His short goatee was so artful, it might as well have been showcased in a museum, which made Isaac wonder about John's sensitive skin and whisker burn and—

He blinked to keep from thinking too much about John with someone else.

Manly roars echoed from inside.

"What exactly is happening in there?" Isaac popped the top off his pumpkin as Cleo stopped scrawling on scrap paper and raised one dark brow—the only evidence she was not a natural redhead.

"Didn't you know? It's Ohio State–Wisconsin day: the one day of the year when Tommy and John actually hate each other."

That sounded dubious. "Really."

"Well, no. It's the one blip in their epic love story, though."

More shouting—only John's voice this time.

"And how long is this going to continue?"

Half the table answered, "Three hours."

Cleo reached her red, manicured fingers into her pumpkin and pulled out seeds and slime. Every handful hit the table with a wet *slop*.

Adam glanced toward the house. "Sometimes, I swear John is straight."

"From what I've heard, you know damn well he isn't," whispered a man in eyeliner. He was incredibly tall and looked vaguely familiar.

Oh. He was one of the drag queens Isaac had seen at the Cave.

Adam cleared his throat and drew on his pumpkin.

"What? Are we not going to talk about the fact that you two fucked? Please. Everyone knows."

"Sasha, don't be a bitch," Cleo snapped and then blushed. "Sorry, Dr. Twain."

He resolutely focused on his pumpkin.

"Boy may have lost some weight over the summer, but thank Christ he didn't lose that tight little ass." Sasha shoved Adam in the shoulder. "I want details."

"No," he said.

Sasha kept going. "I bet he's a power bottom. Boy can probably work that mouth."

Adam glared. "Enough."

Isaac channeled his emotions into his pumpkin. Was he angry? No, why would he be angry? John wasn't sleeping with Adam—again—and so what if other men appreciated John?

He was smart and sexy as hell and maybe even a little dangerous. There was plenty to appreciate, and Isaac *appreciated* as often as he could, unlike the other men at the table, so what was there to be angry about?

"Are you going to see him again?" Sasha asked.

Adam gestured toward the house. "I see him right now."

"You know what I mean."

"No, it was a one-time thing, and we are just friends. I'm not even his type; you know that." Adam tossed his knife on the table. "If anyone around here is John's type, it's Isaac. Honey, if you were gay, he would climb you like a tree."

Isaac saw red, not from emotion but from a slip of the knife. "Shit." He'd chopped right into his finger.

Cleo moved to stand. "Dr. Twain?"

"I'm fine." He hurried inside, cradling his bleeding hand.

In a trim, red Wisconsin jersey, John glanced away from the TV when Isaac entered. On his feet immediately, he dragged Isaac into the kitchen and turned on the cold water.

Isaac hissed.

Standing next to each other, John took Isaac's hand and gently rinsed the blood away. "Let me see." He looked closer. "Knew I should have bought the little plastic kid knives."

"It's really nothing."

John kept Isaac's hand under the water and didn't let go, fingers rubbing, massaging while football played in the living room. "You doing okay out there?"

"Adam's not so bad."

John smiled down at their joined hands. "No. He isn't. I hope you don't mind that he's here."

"He's a friend of yours. I don't mind." Making sure Tommy was otherwise engaged, Isaac leaned his nose against John's forehead. "He said you'd climb me like a tree if I were gay."

John nudged him away. "Cut it out."

Isaac stole a quick kiss. "Mm. You taste…" He stole another. "Sweet."

"It's the cloves," John said. "Now, behave."

Isaac wanted to be very bad indeed, but he stood up straight at the sound of someone nearby. Tommy eyed them from a few feet away, shaking his beer to indicate its emptiness. "Do we need an ambulance? Put a finger on ice?"

John turned off the water and grabbed paper towels. "I think the patient will live." He wrapped Isaac's hand and squeezed. "I'll get some Band-Aids from the bathroom. Tommy, don't you dare turn him into an Ohio State fan."

Tommy grinned. "Join the dark side."

For someone who didn't like football, Isaac spent the next two hours thoroughly entertained, his bloody pumpkin forgotten. John and Tommy jumped on furniture, as usual. They cussed out refs. They cussed out coaches. They drank beer after pumpkin beer. At one point, John actually curled into a ball on the floor until Tommy scooped him up and shook him like an Etch-A-Sketch. The game was close, each score answered and defensive play matched.

When it came down to the big finish, it looked like Ohio State might pull off the win. Even though Wisconsin was up by a field goal, OSU lined up for a possible touchdown with only a minute left—which was when John started singing something about "varsity."

"No, you don't." Tommy wrapped him in a bear hug from behind and covered his mouth. They remained like that, tangled together, as players moved on screen. The clock ran, and the pumpkin carvers observed from the sliding glass door.

The quarterback dropped back, back...and Ohio State threw an interception.

Even Tommy's hand over John's mouth could not subdue the victory howl. Tommy let him go and crumbled to his knees, head in his hands.

"Yes!" John roared. His voice was probably heard all the way down on campus.

Everyone but Tommy looked pleased as John doled out high five after high five. Isaac wanted to lift him on his shoulders but refrained, accepting a wink and a smile instead. Then, John knelt by his best friend. They talked quietly together as fans rejoiced on TV.

"You just ruined my season," Tommy said.

"I know."

"And you're happy about it."

John fought a smile. "I love you?"

Tommy shoved him, and John landed on his back, smiling.

As though summoned, Cleo arrived with two shots. "Drink on it, you maniacs."

John lifted his glass. "Best friends forever?"

Tommy toasted. "I hate you."

AFTER THE GAME, revelry commenced in earnest. John was the king of the food spread, an appetizer artist. Isaac still wasn't sure whom to thank for John's culinary side. He suspected the French mother, especially when John pronounced certain dishes with an accent. Her European metabolism might also explain how John stayed so thin.

With drinking and eating came a pleasant haze, only multiplied by the glow of smiling pumpkin faces in the backyard and the chill music from John's stereo. Then, about nine—that was when Isaac got himself into trouble.

He was just standing there, innocently, talking with Adam and Tommy about...something. He couldn't remember what, because he wasn't listening anyway. He watched John laugh and poke a stick into a crackling fire. John caught him looking and went inside. A minute later, Isaac's phone vibrated with a text. *Go home. You're looking at me too much. Come back at eleven.* So Isaac went home and waited, head leaned back on his couch, and tried not to think about what he wanted to do to John in bed—John, who he'd left sort of drunk and smiling on his front porch up the hill.

A vibration roused him. He glanced at the kitchen clock: 10:45. Isaac hadn't even noticed he'd fallen asleep. He rubbed his eyes and looked down at his phone, expecting perhaps an early invite from John. Instead, he lurched up to standing, throat closed on a panicked breath.

It was a text from Simon—*Found you*—along with a picture of Isaac standing behind John at the Ohioana Literary Festival in Columbus. Simon had used some cell phone trick to draw a bright red smiley face over John's eyes and mouth.

Isaac ran up the hill like a man possessed. None of his fear made sense, of course. Simon didn't know John was Isaac's paramour. Even if he did, Simon wouldn't physically hurt John, regardless of what he knew. Simon may have been in the occasional good ole boy bar brawl, but he wasn't violent. Well, he hadn't been violent in Charleston, but that was before Isaac had disappeared from their apartment in July without a word.

Isaac barreled through John's front door, unlocked, as always. "John?"

"Kitchen," came the calm reply. The rest of the house was quiet.

"John, I—" He turned the corner and stopped. His cell phone, clutched in his hand since the message from Simon, hit the floor. "Holy..."

Reclined on the island in nothing but skintight boxer briefs and what appeared to be honey was John, reading an aged collection of Anais Nin erotica. He licked a spoon, which only barely distracted from the way his neck, upper chest, and abdomen glittered with stripes of amber. He lifted his head a little and smiled, dark hair spread behind him in waves. "I spilled some. Can you help?"

Isaac cleared his throat and tried not to just lunge and *take*. "John, we need to talk. I..." He sighed when John sucked the spoon into his mouth once more before setting it on the island by his head.

"No talking. I've had the perfect day, and it's only getting better."

Isaac rested his hands on the edge of the counter. His eyes devoured. John was so long—easy to overlook due to his small frame—but legs, arms, fingers, neck were long, long, and covered in sticky sweet. Isaac leaned down and licked across John's left nipple. John gasped and dropped the book on the floor. His skin smelled like a bonfire and tasted sweet but oaky with maybe orange?

"This is the best honey I've ever tasted," Isaac said.

"Local. Raw. Good for allergies." His fingers barely had time to tangle in Isaac's hair before Isaac pulled his shirt off over his head. He climbed up on the island, straddling John's hips and licked from his belly button to the bottom of his sternum. John whispered his name.

When John again reached for Isaac's hair, Isaac wrapped his fingers around John's slender wrists and pinned them above his head before leaning down to lick the center of his chest. "See? This is where a bit of rope would really come in handy."

"Ha. Nope." John almost sounded stern. "One of my hard limits."

"Yeah? What else?" He sucked a nipple into his mouth.

"Fuck," John moaned. "No reading Stephen King before bed?"

Isaac rolled his jean-clad hips back and forth over John's erection. He pressed John's wrists together and held them both in one hand, loving he could do such a thing.

John struggled for a second, testing the grip, before wilting back onto the cool countertop. A large dollop of warm gold had settled in the crevice at the base of John's neck, so Isaac sucked.

"You love that part of my body," John muttered. "That little inch of me."

Isaac sat back, eyes darting over John's face, which was decidedly more flushed than when Isaac had first arrived. "I've never had this," he said.

"Food foreplay?"

No, that wasn't what he meant. He shook his head and collected some honey from John's chest on his thumb. He wiped his thumb over John's bottom lip until it shined, then leaned forward and pulled the lip into his mouth. John sighed and arched up to meet him, one of his hands still pinned to the island. His other hand pressed against Isaac's lower back, beckoning him closer.

John spoke into his mouth: "Don't you waste a drop."

ISAAC WOKE TO the sound of footsteps on carpet. He moaned and rolled over just as the bed sank at his side. "Hey." John's hand on his bare chest—yes, he knew its exact weight and shape. Isaac opened his eyes to find John dressed in a button-down and blazer. He might have showered, but he hadn't washed his hair. It stood up more on one side than the other, although it still managed to carry that perfect curl. Isaac knew John actually owned a shower cap that he hid under the sink for just such mornings when "doing his hair" took too long.

He cupped John's cheek in his hand. "Where are you going?"

"Church with Cleo."

Isaac yawned and stretched. "You don't go to church."

"I do sometimes. I like the music."

Isaac caressed one of John's thick eyebrows. "Did you know all the hair on your body is above your nose?"

"Not *all* of it." He smiled and shared a kiss. His mouth tasted like mint.

Isaac tried to finger comb John's hair into symmetry, but John winced when one of his fingers got stuck—and stayed stuck. "You have honey in your hair."

John leaned into the tug. "Maybe I should have washed it this morning."

Isaac sat up and sucked the ends of John's hair into his mouth. "Tasty." He further tried to suck on John's mouth, but John shoved him away with that familiar hand on his chest.

"Nope. Church."

Isaac fell back on the bed but overtly put his hand down the front of his boxers.

John rolled his eyes and stood. "Fucking menace. Be back in two hours or so."

"Pray for us sinners!" Isaac shouted at John's retreating back.

"It's not that kind of church!" The front door opened and closed tight.

Isaac eventually got up and took a hot shower, mindful to wash away any lingering traces of honey from the night before. He thought about throwing John's sheets in the washer too. They had to be ruined, considering once they'd finally finished, they'd both been covered in tacky residue. But coffee first.

He pulled on a pair of pajama bottoms he kept at John's—considering John's were laughably too small—and hummed his way to the kitchen. He smiled when he noticed the half-empty jar of honey on the counter and went to work boiling water.

John's front door opened and shut, but it had only been twenty minutes since he'd left. Isaac almost called his name but heard heavy footsteps in the hall, so not John. Before Isaac could make a dash for a closet, Tommy appeared in the doorway—and froze.

IT WAS A small, packed diner on Union Street in the center of town. Isaac walked past it every day—the long, thin, silver box that resembled an alien spaceship on the predominantly brick block. Around them, couples and families laughed, chatted, and stuffed their faces with piles of potato and egg. Tommy did nothing but glare, even when the waitress poured two steaming cups of coffee into waiting mugs.

Tommy sipped. "Do you know who makes the best cup of coffee in Lothos?"

"John."

"That's right. John. He uses some secret French magic."

"It's cinnamon," Isaac said, stock still, not reaching for his own mug.

Of all the things that had happened so far—the kitchen stare, the hurry to get dressed, the tense walk down the hill—Tommy had yet to look this angry, and it was simply because Isaac knew John well enough to know a secret.

"You're straight," Tommy said.

"I was."

"And what, you meet John Conlon and think, 'Hmm, I'd like to try dick?'"

Isaac thanked God the restaurant was so damn loud. "No. I've always been gay. I was just married to a woman for a long time."

Tommy leaned so close, Isaac could see every speck of dirt on his glasses. "How long?"

"Ten years."

"No. How long have you been fucking John?"

When the waitress moved to come closer, Isaac held up his hand and shook his head. They would not be eating breakfast anytime soon.

"How long, Isaac?"

"Since Barcelona." Seemed like a million years ago. He couldn't remember a time when he didn't know the sounds John made in his sleep.

"Great. Yeah, that's great." Tommy turned his rolled silverware over and back. "Make possibly career-destroying decisions on a night when the whole world is a shit show."

"I kissed him in Columbus." He didn't know why he was trying to defend himself—defend them. As John had said, the catalyst hadn't been the shooting. Well, maybe it had been the breaking point, but Isaac had wanted John long before that night and now knew the feeling was mutual.

Tommy leaned his elbows on the table. "You have to break it off."

"What?" The back of his hands tingled.

"Isaac." Tommy shoved the forgotten coffee out of the way. "You will not get him fired. This city, the school... He loves them both way too much to lose them."

"It's not my decision."

A waitress nearby dropped a stack of plates. Tommy closed his eyes tight and took a deep breath through his nose. "It needs to be your decision. You know why? The most amazing thing about John is his incredible lack of self-preservation. He doesn't even lock his goddamn front door." It would have been easier if Tommy had been yelling. Instead, he whispered, rage evident in the lines around his mouth. "John would do anything to help someone, to save them. Did I know he was going to step in front of a gun last year? No, but maybe I should have. Maybe I should have tackled him and not Cleo. Instead, I sat there and watched my best friend…" He shook his head and looked outside. "When Chris pressed that gun to his throat, I thought, 'This is it. No more football. No more laughs. No more John.' I was prepared to never see him again. But he lived. Somehow. He had a bruise for a week." Tommy pointed to the base of his own neck. "I couldn't stop staring at it. All the shit going on around us the week after, and that fucking bruise is what haunts me most because it could have been a hole. He has lost so much. Please don't take anything else."

A child cried in a booth nearby.

Isaac felt cold, so he wrapped his palms around his coffee mug. "It'll hurt him. If I break it off, I think it'll hurt him a lot."

Tommy sighed through his nose. "He knows better than this."

"Maybe not this year. Maybe he's trying to feel alive."

"Yeah, join the club."

"I did." Isaac glanced at the bear-shaped honey bottle on the table. "That's why I'm here. Maybe that's why I'm with John."

"He's not a defibrillator."

"No. But, Tommy, we make each other happy."

Tommy shook his head. "I don't trust you with him."

"Why?"

"You're quiet. Quiet people have secrets. Have you told him all of yours?"

Isaac leaned back in his chair but didn't lose eye contact with Tommy, who might as well have been an oversized child with his Hambden hoodie, acne scars, and jeans—but who saw right through Isaac, even more so than John.

Tommy didn't wait for his answer. "I knew it."

"John has secrets too. The time needs to be right for us to talk about them."

"If you hurt him, I'll kill you." He pushed back from the table and threw a couple dollar bills between their full coffee cups.

"Where are you going?" Isaac didn't move, but his words made Tommy spin back around on the squeaky heel of his sneaker.

"*We* are going back to John's. I only dragged you to this shitty diner because I was less likely to punch you in the face in public." He sniffed. "Come on. I'd like to be there when he gets back as John and I will be having an unpleasantly extensive conversation."

They didn't beat John home. In fact, John looked sort of panicked when they walked in, probably because Isaac had disappeared and left his cell phone behind. Then, he saw Tommy...and Isaac...Tommy.

"Oh, shit," he muttered and closed his eyes.

"You are in so much trouble." Tommy stomped through the kitchen. "Make me a cup of that magic coffee of yours and meet me outside. Bring a blanket so your skinny ass doesn't catch cold. Isaac, go home."

"But—"

"No." Tommy looked at Isaac but pointed at John. "My best friend. Our shit. You'll see him tomorrow. Chop, chop, French boy. *Cinnamon.* Goddamn it." He continued cussing out onto the back porch, the orange leaves in direct contrast to the blue sky overhead.

Isaac didn't dare show affection with Tommy so close, for fear the guy might actually beat him to a pulp. He just shrugged at John instead. "Tomorrow? I have something I need to talk to you about."

"Ominous."

"Maybe a little."

John ran a hand through his hair. "Excellent."

He put one hand on John's elbow. "It's not about us. I made it clear to Tommy I'm not giving you up."

He tapped his fingers on the kitchen island. "You hardly know me."

Isaac snorted. "Yeah. I do."

"Lunch tomorrow? Talk then?"

"Let's make it dinner at my place," Isaac said.

"*Super* ominous."

Isaac grabbed his hand before he could reach the sink. "I can't imagine my life without you in it."

John was about to say something, but Tommy's voice screaming, "Coffee, Conlon!" cut him right off.

"Get out of here before he goes for the kitchen knives."

Isaac kissed him on the cheek and made the short walk home, slowly, deliberately. As soon as he got there, he put on his running clothes and shoes and ran farther than he ever had before, stumbling upon a decaying cemetery on the edge of town, overwrought with long grass and fallen leaves. A weeping angel towered above it all. Isaac rested his hand on the abrasive old marble, stained with creeping green moss, and marveled over how much he inexplicably had to lose.

Chapter Ten

WONDER OF WONDERS, Isaac felt fully engaged in class Monday morning, possibly because—for once—one of his young composition students showed promise as she read her short essay about creative process. For but a moment, he remembered what it was like to teach and to love it. He'd had a taste of it at the *Being Frank* meetings, but to find it in class was a much-needed, pleasant surprise, especially with the looming promise of a dinner with John that could go badly. Very badly. John wasn't going to like learning about Simon, but Tommy was right: secrets weren't good. Secrets had ruined Isaac's marriage. They wouldn't ruin what he had with John.

At the hour's close, kids scrambled to their next classes, maybe lunch. As usual, no one ever stuck around to chat. Once they'd gone, Isaac collected his own bag and planned a brief respite at Donkey where he wanted to think things through. He had a lot to explain that night, and none of it painted Isaac in a positive light. He might as well be prepared.

Preoccupied, he almost ran straight into someone on his way through the door. He stopped, backed up. "Sorry."

"Isaac."

In the half-second it took for Isaac to lift his head, Simon had already shoved him back into the classroom. The big desk up front jerked as their bodies made contact, as would be expected with the sudden, violent arrival of four hundred pounds of combined male. Simon threw the first punch, but Isaac didn't retaliate. He played defense, even when they knocked over desks in the front row and Isaac tasted blood.

A flurry of familiar movement—Simon included—interrupted the impromptu beat down. John and Tommy were there, yelling and pulling. Isaac tried to sit up and make some announcement, but what the hell was he supposed to say?

With the addition of John and Tommy's weight on his back, Simon tumbled backward, still kicking. What caught all their attention was the hollow *bang* of John's head against the big metal desk up front.

The scuffling stopped, replaced by glances of concern, even from Simon, who held out a hand to help John to his feet.

Ignoring the offer, John said, "Damn it," with his hand on the back of his head. Most of his hair was in his eyes.

"Are you okay?" Tommy asked.

"No." The snappy delivery was less of pain, more of irritation. John shoved his hair out of his face, gaze moving to the open door, where students congregated, mouths wide. He dragged himself to his feet and closed the door but not before nodding to Janelle, who glared at Simon as if he'd insulted Nine Inch Nails.

Isaac remained on his ass, tasting blood. The skin beneath his eye ached and felt wet. He endured the pain, wanted it, because physical pain was preferable to the emotional upheaval that had just walked through his classroom door.

John took steps toward him, but Tommy thwarted his approach by placing his own body between them, glaring at both Isaac and Simon in turn. Still, John looked over his friend's shoulder to ask, "Isaac, are you all right?"

He had no idea how to answer that question.

Simon stood, brushing off khakis and a blue sweater. "Apologies for your head."

John cussed under his breath. "Jesus, man, who the hell are you?"

"I'm Simon. Isaac's boyfriend."

Isaac pushed to stand and stuttered a few nonsensical syllables as John's shoulders curled forward. He lost three inches of height.

Meanwhile, Tommy growled, "What?"

"Simon—"

Ignoring Isaac's plea, Simon turned to John and Tommy. "Would you gentlemen excuse us?"

John said, "I'm not going fucking anywhere."

Isaac didn't know who was more terrifying in that moment: Simon with his outward, physical rage or John with the simmering storm that reflected like lightning in his eyes.

"Mr. Simon person." Tommy held his hands out as if they held invisible plates. "Go on."

Facing Isaac, Simon wielded his slow, Southern drawl like a weapon. "Did you think I would give up? Think I wouldn't find you? I admit, damn sneaky of you to keep your name off the Hambden University website, but then, there you were, standing behind Mr. John Conlon at some literary festival. The hero professor." The light from outside made his blue eyes burn. "Easy to find you then."

Isaac held his hands up. "I'm sorry for—"

"For what? Disappearing off the face of the earth? You could have been dead, Isaac. Nobody knew what happened to you, not even Elizabeth."

His stomach twisted at the mention of her name. "You talked to Elizabeth?"

"Of course, I talked to Elizabeth, and she was not very happy to see me." He clasped his hands into fists. "Why the hell would she wanna see the man who helped destroy her marriage?"

Isaac took a single step away. "Why don't you just calm down?"

"Calm down?" Simon lifted a chair and hurled it against the wall.

The ricochet sounded like a gun. Tommy only tensed, but John covered his ears and closed his eyes. He curled forward farther, so Isaac rushed to him.

"John." He put his hands on his shoulders. "John, you're okay. You're safe."

Tommy forcefully elbowed Isaac away. "Bullshit, he is."

Tommy stared him down, but soon, Isaac felt another pair of eyes on him—or, more accurately, on John, who'd calmed enough to realize they weren't on College Green in June waiting to die. Simon stared at John, and John stared back. His eyes were wide, and most of his weight looked to be on the heels of his Converse shoes, ready to run.

"Oh, my God, he's fucking you," Simon said.

"Simon, let's go outside." Isaac reached for his ex-lover's shoulder, only to be batted away.

"Look at him, Isaac." He studied John inch by inch. "He's not what you like. You like big guys. You like it rough. Jesus, does he cry when you fuck him?"

Tommy shoved Simon in the shoulder. "Watch your mouth."

"I guess he does have a nice mouth, doesn't he, Isaac? Wonder what he can do with it?"

"Probably a lot more than you," John said, and Simon lurched forward. Both Tommy and Isaac got in his way.

Calmly, John walked right up to the flailing fighter—who had a good five inches on him—and said, "You want to fight me right now? You're two times my size. What the fuck is that going to prove, asshole?"

And Simon wilted, misplaced anger gone. Tommy and Isaac let him go.

"Fuck you," John said quietly. "And fuck you, too, Isaac." He left the classroom, Tommy right behind.

"What he said," Tommy muttered, and for the first time in over a month, Isaac remembered the cold emptiness of despair.

ISAAC CANCELED HIS afternoon classes and took Simon to a quiet booth in the back of Crocodile Lounge, close enough to his own apartment in case they started screaming at each other, but not literally inside Isaac's place. He didn't want Simon to know where he lived. The restaurant, hopping and filled with colored light and music at night, was pretty dead right then since they didn't serve lunch—but they did serve booze.

They both ordered whiskey; no matter that it was only lunchtime.

"So what happened?" Simon asked. "You moved up here and shacked up?"

"No. I never intended to meet John."

"Ain't that sweet?" His breath shuddered, and the angry slam of his glass against the table distracted from the wet red of his eyes. "Wouldn't one—or both—of you get fired if word got out that you were fucking?"

"Don't hurt John because of something I've done."

He shrugged and wiped at his eyes. "I don't know, Isaac, it looks like hurting him is just the way to get to you."

"You wouldn't. You aren't like that."

Simon leaned forward in his seat. Isaac hadn't noticed earlier, but he smelled like fast food and smoke. His hand shook, pointed in Isaac's face. "How do you know how I am right now? Do you know what I've been through, how scared I've been?"

The waitress made eye contact, and for the second time in two days, Isaac had to shoot a glare that quite clearly said, "Do not come over here." She already seemed hesitant considering the bloody, bruised state of his face.

Simon continued, "The man I love, the man I *waited for*, finally left his wife. We had a place all picked out. We were going to start our life together." He choked out a single sob and hid his face behind his huge hands. "You broke my heart and abandoned me, Isaac. You disappeared!"

Isaac finished his first drink. Maybe he did need the waitress after all. "I had to leave. The apartment reminded me of all the things I'd done wrong."

"Am I one of those things?" Usually blindingly handsome, the skin beneath Simon's eyes sagged. His square jaw was painted black—probably hadn't shaved in days—and his hair, typically close-cropped, tickled the tops of his ears.

"It was wrong," Isaac said.

"It never felt wrong to me."

"I was cheating on my wife."

"Yeah, well, now you're cheating on *me* with..." Simon laughed through tears. "Hell of a competition, Isaac. I mean to say, I've never stepped in front of a bullet before, and I sure don't have that hair."

"John has nothing to do with this."

"Come back to Charleston, and I won't make a fuss."

Isaac tried to get as far away from Simon as the booth would allow. "What's there to make a fuss about?"

"You and John. I'll ruin him. Promise."

He shook his head. "You have no evidence of anything. People don't even know I'm gay."

"I'm a lawyer, Isaac. You think I can't find a way?"

How could one of the most eligible men in Charleston look so ugly?

They'd met at a drag night on one of Isaac's rare bar visits. They hadn't even exchanged names before hitting the back alley. Only later would Isaac realize he'd accidentally fucked one of the most infamous Southern boys in town: a divorce lawyer who struck fear into the hearts of cheating, rich men. The irony was thicker than swamp mud, especially when Isaac went through his own divorce a year later and refused Simon's help.

"What's it going to be?"

"I need time," Isaac said.

"For what?"

He hissed, "I have a life here, Simon."

Simon tilted his head. The side of his right eye crinkled as his closed-lipped mouth turned up in a semblance of smile. Isaac had seen him make that face before in court. "You mean *him*."

"I have a job. I was a last minute emergency hire. The school needs me."

"I don't give a fuck about the school. What about me? Us?"

His fist tightened on his empty glass. "You are not endearing yourself to me right now."

"Oh, this isn't me, Isaac." Simon pointed at himself. "This is what you did. Once we go home, everything can go back to the way it was, but right now, you're dealing with Isaac Twain's creature. Jesus, I've been so busy thinking about you, I'm about to lose my job. I haven't been able to focus on anything, not knowing what happened to you, the man I..." He pushed his hands through his black hair and used a bar napkin to wipe his face. "I can't do this right now. I've been driving a day and a night to find you, and I just need sleep before I lose my damn mind."

"You're not staying at my place."

"No, I'm not. The last thing I need is to smell him on your sheets."

John was everywhere in Isaac's apartment, from a Wisconsin coffee mug to his preferred lube.

Simon slid from the booth, unsteady on his feet, surely from exhaustion, lack of food, and the addition of alcohol. "I'm getting a hotel, but don't think I'm going away." He didn't bother throwing money on the table.

JOHN WASN'T ANSWERING his phone. Of course he wasn't, but Cleo was. Despite being the administrative head of everything English—and the gossip guru—she hadn't heard about the altercation in Ellis Hall. Yet. What a miracle. She answered his questions with her usual flighty innocence: *Yes, John is in class. Why wouldn't John be in class? Isaac, is everything okay?*

Isaac gave him time, gave him space, to pass through his Monday without further interruption, but once dinnertime hit, he walked straight to John's house and didn't bother knocking.

John sat on his living room couch, TV black, no music for once. The house had never felt so menacing. An orange pill bottle held court with a half-empty bottle of scotch on the coffee table.

"How many pills did you take?"

"Just a half." He didn't make eye contact. "Helps with the buzz."

"You shouldn't mix anxiety meds and alcohol."

John smiled with zero amusement. "You're going to give me advice right now?"

He sighed.

"Your face looks like shit."

Isaac knew and didn't care.

"So when are you moving back to Charleston?"

"What?"

"Well, that's why he's here, right? To get you back." Apparently annoyed with the empty glass in his hand, John grabbed the scotch bottle and took a loud gulp. "It's no big deal, so go to him. We were just fucking."

Isaac felt his pulse in his head. "Is that what you think this is? We're just fucking?"

"You have no right to get angry at me right now."

"This is not just fucking," Isaac yelled.

"But it is a lie!" John stood and shoved him in the chest.

"I never lied to you."

"You've been lying by omission since the day we met! 'Yeah, I was married to a woman, but I'd love to suck your dick. I didn't just *leave* Charleston; I fucking disappeared, and oh, yeah, I have a boyfriend!'"

Isaac reached out to touch, and John reared back.

"Don't you dare. I have had a headache all fucking day because some jackass rammed my skull against a desk.

Being touched by another jackass is the last thing I want right now."

"I didn't lie. I didn't...want to lie." Isaac folded his arms to keep from reaching out and fixing the beautiful mess of John's hair. "What happened to me at Broad destroyed me. It made me so scared to be open about my sexuality, scared to let myself be happy, so when I met you, I did not plan...this. That's why I never told you about Simon. I didn't realize we...that I..."

"Use your fucking words."

"I didn't realize I was going to fall in love with you."

John's gasp turned into a quiet bawl, so Isaac reached for him, but John slapped his hand away. "Don't."

Isaac reached again, took hold of his wrists, and John fought hard to get away, curving his arms this way and that to escape Isaac's hold.

"Let go," John said.

"I can't."

John gave one more valiant effort to disentangle their bodies, out of breath with the futility of escaping someone much stronger—and someone terrified of letting go.

"John." Isaac's voice shook. "Please."

John expunged a heaving breath before folding the top of his head against Isaac's chest, and Isaac finally let go of his wrists. John's shoulders shook as he clawed at Isaac's shirt. "Today hurt so much." He sobbed.

"I'm sorry. I'm so sorry." Isaac lifted John's face and kissed his forehead, his tear-streaked cheeks.

"Don't ever hurt me like that again."

"I won't. I'm sorry." He wrapped John in his arms and held him until the crying stopped.

Back on the couch, John tended to Isaac's wounds. Well, wound. His bottom lip was split, but there was nothing to be done for it. The cut under his eye, though, needed looking after. John used an alcohol swab to poke and prod.

"I'm sorry about the things Simon said today."

John shrugged. So close, his breath smelled like vanilla and peat. "I know I'm not your type, Isaac. It's no big deal."

"You are literally my only type right now."

John smiled—maybe a little. "That's just because you *love* me."

"I do. But there is some bad news."

"Oh, goody." John reached for a butterfly bandage. "I love bad news."

"Simon is threatening our jobs."

"Original." He peeled back the sticky sides and gently pressed the bandage to Isaac's face.

"We need to lie low for a little while. Not see each other. Simon is going to try to get evidence that we're...*us*, so only official stuff. School stuff. We can't go to each other's houses."

"You're at my house right now."

"And Simon is asleep at a hotel."

John trailed his fingers down the edge of Isaac's jaw. "Should I be scared of him?"

"No. He's a good guy. I just fucked up."

"Yeah. You did." He kissed Isaac's cheek. "Go home."

"I don't know if I'll be able to sleep without you."

John shook his head. "You don't deserve to sleep with me right now."

John walked Isaac out, but the door closed behind him with an echoing finality—especially when the lock clicked. It was the first time Isaac had ever known John to lock his front door.

Chapter Eleven

WIND WHIPPED THE candles dead on College Green's altar as Isaac swept past, late for the Tuesday night *Being Frank* meeting. Between classes, he and Simon had spent much of the afternoon talking in coffee shops and bars. Well, arguing. Mostly arguing. All he wanted was to wrap himself in John's sheets and sleep cuddled together, but that was impossible for now. For the time being, they could barely look at each other.

He was out of breath by the time he reached Ellis Hall's third floor. Thanks to the aging heaters, the whole place smelled like farts. He tore off his coat, too hot, as he walked down the hall to the sound of shouting. By the time he reached the classroom, he recognized the voices: Anthony and Janelle.

"This isn't a political journal," Anthony said. He'd shoved his Afro under a hat but looked ready to set his hair free and start tugging.

Janelle gestured to her computer. "It's a well-written piece."

"Yeah, about gun control!"

John didn't even look up when Isaac walked in. He stood, leaned against the chalkboard with his arms crossed. Mouth turned down, his green eyes stared straight ahead—glazed, unseeing.

"Janelle. Girlfriend. Listen to me. We are not here to make political statements. We can't publish a treatise on gun reform. We need art, not politics."

Janelle, a little thing, seemed huge when she stood and got right in his face. "No, we need truth, and the truth is none of this shit would have happened if Chris hadn't been able to buy a gun."

Isaac waited for John to step in, but he didn't. He just stood there, as did the literary magazine staff, frozen like nervous-looking ice sculptures.

"I'm not arguing that with you, but this piece has no place in a literary journal!"

Janelle flailed her hand, black bracelets clicking. "And the one you like does? Who cares what that psycho was thinking? John?"

He didn't move.

"See, nobody cares!" she shouted.

"Are you even listening to yourself right now?" Anthony asked. "You named this literary magazine *Being Frank* because you wanted even Chris to have a voice because he's dead, too, and he was our friend."

"Hey," Isaac said, but no one listened. John didn't even look like he paid attention—John, who was usually so good at fixing things.

"Fuck Chris Frank," Janelle said. "Forget about him. Forget the whole stupid thing."

Anthony hit the desk with his fist, which at least made John flinch. "You wouldn't be saying any of this shit if you weren't so drunk all the time!"

"Enough," Isaac yelled. "Anthony, Janelle, hallway. Now." He threw his bag on the floor and didn't wait.

Out in the hall, two of the most talented kids in the entire English Department looked like bombs ready to blow. Janelle violently chewed her thumbnail. A bit of her purple lipstick had smeared onto the side of her cheek, and old mascara melted under her eyes. Anthony tapped his foot until Janelle snapped at him to stop.

"What's the matter with you two?" Isaac asked.

"What's the matter with you?" Janelle spat. "Why are you getting into fistfights in classrooms? Your eye looks like shit, by the way."

Isaac lifted a finger. "Watch it. I'm still your teacher."

"Oh, fuck you." She stomped down the hall.

"Janelle, get back here." He'd never felt so much like a disrespected parent. "Anthony, talk to me."

Anthony sighed, anger wilted like a wet flower. "It's not you, Dr. Twain. It's not me either. I don't know why I let her get to me today." He toed at linoleum. "It's Demi's birthday Thursday. Well, it would have been. Janelle isn't doing all right."

"Is she on antidepressants or anything?"

"Yeah. And she sees some head doctor." He shrugged. "But she's drinking so much, man. I get worried, then I get scared, then I get angry. You just saw angry."

"Does John know about Demi's birthday?"

Anthony scoffed. "Yeah, man, but..." He waved into the classroom where John looked like he barely breathed. "I had him this morning in class. He's been like this all day. He won't even, like, acknowledge my presence. Is he okay?" Exaggerated shrug. "I don't know. It's like everyone's gone crazy."

"All right, I'm going to cancel the meeting tonight. I think we've seen enough."

"Sure, but, I mean, Janelle makes a good point that we're going to have to discuss. Do we have an agenda? Is *Being Frank* a platform of some kind, or are we just looking for beautiful, emotional work?"

Isaac pressed his lips together, considering. "Say what you just said to me to them, and we'll vote on it next week."

"All right. Can you see if John's all right? He's freaking me out, man."

Isaac nodded, although he had no right to question John's mental health. God, he was probably the cause of the blank, hopeless look on his face.

Isaac dismissed the students after Anthony made his announcement, most of them rushing to get out the door. The whole room stank of tension with just a touch of John's witch hazel lotion. When Isaac tried to approach the stock-still creative writing professor, John shook his head. "Just go home, Isaac."

Broken-hearted, he texted John as he walked.

Do you know it's Demi's birthday Thursday? I don't think Janelle should be alone.

John responded, *She won't be. Classes all day, and Anthony will stay at her place overnight. A bunch of us are going out to dinner for Demi.*

Isaac crossed Union in the direction of his apartment and was about to reply when—

You can come, if you want.

I would love to, Isaac texted.

To be close to John, to see John, to maybe make John laugh just once. When was the last time he'd seen him laugh—really laugh—not the armored chuckle he used to deflect?

I miss you, John texted.

Isaac stopped on the sidewalk and tried to keep the punch of emotion from knocking him over. *I miss you so much.*

As if they hadn't just seen each other. He would definitely need a long run that night.

He opened the door to his stairwell and took the steps two at a time only to find his front door open, the lock busted. Slivers of wood decorated the tiny, carpeted foyer, and Simon sat stretched out on his couch.

"What the hell?" Isaac said.

Simon drank whiskey—a bottle of expensive Japanese stuff John had brought over. "There is an awful lot of John Conlon hair in your shower." He leaned his head back, eyes closed as though so very relaxed when his entire body screamed pent-up unease. "Not like I'm building a court case or anything. Hell, if you wanted to right now, you could probably get me disbarred—not that I give a shit anymore. Just saying, you used to be so much more careful. I couldn't even be seen at your house, and now, you're letting him stay here, shower here. He must feel real special."

"I should call the police. And get you disbarred."

Simon guffawed. "Yeah. Sure. Go ahead. I'll make all sorts of noise if you do."

"How do you know where I live?"

"Nice redheaded girl at your office." He took a long gulp of whiskey from the bottle. "Told her I was an old friend, here to surprise you. Wasn't she the sweetest? Didn't know there were so many pretty, little things in Ohio."

Isaac grabbed the bottle away from him. "Get out."

"He went to Wisconsin, huh?"

Must have noticed the coffee mug.

Isaac said, "Stop making this about John."

Simon crossed his shiny dress shoes on the coffee table. He always wore dress shoes, even now, when his clothes were a wreck and his black hair a mess in the back. "We've been talking in circles all day, Isaac. The thing that puts me at a loss is that I didn't do anything to deserve your hate."

Isaac shook his head. "I don't hate you."

"Really? You abandoned me, and now, you're treating me like a stranger. You haven't held me, kissed me. It doesn't make me sad; it makes me livid." His lip twitched, revealing his teeth. "Variables may have changed—geography and time—but those shouldn't be enough to make you stop loving me. No, the biggest change is him, so I need to get rid of him."

Isaac gawked. "Are you even listening to yourself?"

"Yes, and now, you need to listen." He stood and poked a finger in Isaac's chest. "I'm gonna tell the school about you and him."

"Please, Simon—"

"Twenty-four hours." His brows wrinkled over bloodshot eyes. "I'm giving you twenty-four hours, and you choose me and we get our life back. Or you choose him and ruin his."

Isaac shook his head. "Either choice I make will ruin him."

Simon took a huge breath and blinked his eyes wide. "Well, it sure is a shame after all he went through last year. I remember all the news coverage. Remember thinking he was cute." With laughter like a cold breeze, he leaned close to Isaac and whispered, "You shouldn't have left me." Then, he was gone. Nothing but the scent of cigarettes betrayed his existence—that and the broken door.

Isaac slumped onto the sofa and finished the bottle of whiskey in twenty minutes. John would joke about being pissed it was gone, but Isaac supposed missing liquor was the least of their worries. Head floating, he stumbled into his bedroom and fell face-first into the pillow. Desperately, he sought to find just a bit of John's sleep scent—that mix of earthiness and night sweat—but nothing. So he cried. He fell asleep gasping on his own snot, head pounding, and eyes burning with salt.

JOHN'S CLASSES STARTED late on Wednesday, so he wasn't in Ellis Hall when Isaac arrived, but Meeks was, waiting by his office door. In an ugly business suit—a puke shade of green this time—she stood, arms crossed, cup of coffee in her hand. He wondered if she ever got headaches from wearing her hair tied back so tight.

"We need to talk." She didn't smile.

He unlocked the door and let her inside.

Meeks sat behind his desk like she owned the place, while Isaac sat in the cheap leather chair usually reserved for students. "I heard there was quite a tiff last night."

Okay, so she was there to talk about the literary magazine, not Monday's brawl. *Breathe.* "How did you know?"

"I don't have spies at your meetings, if that's what you're asking. I have concerned students who have a right to be after last year."

"It wasn't like that."

The chair squeaked when she leaned back into a tiny sliver of sun. "Janelle has always been unstable. Demi kept her in check. Now, it seems Anthony is doing his best to fill the void, but I still worry."

Isaac folded his hands in his lap. "How nice of you."

She grinned, shifting the too-much makeup on her face in a parody of emotion. "I know you don't think very highly of me, Dr. Twain. I don't think very highly of myself most days. I didn't even want this job, but with Abby dead, I was most qualified. So now, I am trying to keep this fractured department together at any cost. I'm not here to make friends." The chair creaked forward. "So, tell me. Do I have anything to worry about with Janelle?"

"I'll have John check in with her."

She clicked her tongue. "Because he's the picture of stability."

"They're close," he snapped. "I think she would tell him if something was wrong."

"No, you're right. I suppose the gays do stick together."

He tried not to look horribly offended.

She poked at some student papers on his desk. "One other thing. I realize Tommy and John are reckless idiots, but aren't you a little old for fistfights?"

Shit.

"Let me guess. Affair with a married woman and her husband found out?"

If only it were so simple. "It's none of your business."

Meeks smiled the way dogs do before they bite. "I'm your boss. Your whole life on campus is my business. Is the problem sorted?"

He thought about resigning right there, saving John the hell that might soon be coming, but he couldn't get the words out. God, he was a coward. "It will be."

"Good. I'm glad you're friends with those madmen, but it would be nice if you could be a positive influence. Someone they can look up to."

"If anyone should be looked up to, it's John."

She studied his face before humming. "We used to be friends, John and I. Good ones. Some would say we shared a similar entertaining 'attitude problem.' Then, Abby died, I became his boss, and we haven't agreed on anything since." She flipped one of Isaac's pens around with her fingertips. "You would tell me if something was wrong with him. Wouldn't you?"

If he was being honest, Meeks was the last person he would tell if he thought something was genuinely wrong with John. She seemed the sort to judge first, listen later, but he agreed just to get her the hell out of his office.

She did stand then, silhouetted against a dark window. The sun had gone, and storms threatened. "Just remember, Dr. Twain, I didn't bring you here to cause trouble. No more on-campus drama. No more canceling classes. Try not to rock the boat."

He nodded again. He was beginning to feel like a very tall bobblehead.

Once she was finally, blessedly gone, he almost broke the damn chair with the force of his slump. It was Elizabeth all over again—divorce, dishonesty, and the loss of everything good.

Like being caught in a waterfall, screaming all the way down.

His phone pinged, and he hoped it would be John, just a single word from John. Of course it was Simon because Isaac was in the waterfall, hurtling toward jagged rock. He landed with a bloody splat when he read *John starting late today?* and opened the attachment: a photo of John's house.

SIMON'S CAR WAS parked outside, South Carolina plates, and Isaac heard the scuffle as soon as he walked in, although it was quiet—just fabric against fabric—until John said, "Stop," and Isaac barreled into the kitchen. Simon had John trapped against the counter, hand buried in his hair and tugging. John's chin pointed to the ceiling, fists pushing into Simon's chest. John had never looked so damn small, and Isaac had never felt so angry.

He took a step closer but stopped when Simon pulled roughly on John's hair. "Not another step, Isaac."

"Simon, just let him go."

John stayed perfectly still except for the rapid rising and falling of his chest, fingers clenched in the front of Simon's shirt.

"I suppose I can see the appeal." He studied John's face. "Someone so delicate, easy to push around. Easy to get a real good grip on his hair."

"Fuck off," John whispered and shoved but might as well have been fighting a wall.

Simon only leaned closer until John was basically crushed against the sink, head tilted at an unnatural angle. "Nice lips. Wonder if they taste sweet." He ducked down as if to give John a kiss, which was when Isaac moved—but apparently John had had quite enough, as well.

Despite being glued together from chest to knee, he managed to scrape a Converse-clad foot down the front of Simon's shin. Simon yelled and fell back, which gave John enough space to punch him in the throat. It wasn't a perfect punch, but it had enough force to make Simon choke and bend forward at the waist. John hid behind Isaac, and Isaac was only so happy to play shield as Simon wheezed.

"Well." Simon laughed with no humor, a cold impression of joy. "Not so easy to push around then. Nice punch, John. Maybe I'll press charges, just for fun."

"You're in my fucking house." His voice shook, so Isaac reached back and grabbed his hand.

"I'm just kidding. I'd be in more trouble than you." Simon rubbed the front of his neck. "We did have a nice chat, though. I told him about the baby, Isaac. Thought he might want to know."

"Get out of my house," John said. "If you ever come back, I'll fucking murder you."

"I might let you." Simon itched his upper lip. His eyes went fuzzy as though his body remained but his mind left the room, revisiting happier times filled with Isaac's now busted promises. He blinked back to reality. "Isaac, I took the liberty of making us dinner reservations for tonight. I'll text you the details." When he circled the island to leave, John noticeably stepped to the opposite side of Isaac. Before leaving, Simon said, "John Conlon. Jesus, I wish it was easier to hate you."

As soon as the front door shut, Isaac reached for John's face. "Are you okay?"

"Yeah. I mean, maybe?"

John had already been dressed for work when Simon arrived, so his light-blue chambray shirt was crooked and untucked under his corduroy blazer. Isaac tugged at both, lining things up, as though in fixing the fabric he could fix the situation.

"I didn't know you knew self-defense," Isaac said.

"I'm a loud-mouthed gay guy who looks like a girl. I've been getting in fights my whole life."

He ran his thumbs across John's cheeks and kissed his forehead again and again. "Why did you let him into your house? What were you thinking?" He tugged John closer and hugged him and kissed him.

"I thought we could talk. Isaac—hey, stop. You're hurting me."

"I…"

"Shh, calm down. Calm down."

He buried his head against John's shoulder and clung.

"Come here." John guided Isaac to his bedroom and lay him down the center of the bed. He curled up at Isaac's side and rested his head on his chest. Together, they breathed, slow and deep. After a long bit of silence that involved nothing but gentle caresses, John said, "The abortion wasn't your fault."

"Yes, it was," Isaac said.

"It was Elizabeth's decision, not yours."

"She made the decision after I told her I was gay and leaving her for a man. If that's not a catalyst, I don't know what is."

John leaned up on his elbow. "You didn't know she was pregnant."

"It doesn't matter. That child isn't here because of me."

"Isaac, what kind of world would you have brought it into?" John asked. "One of lies and infidelity where kids shoot each other?"

He pulled John's face down and kissed both his cheeks. Isaac wanted to bathe in the familiar scent. "Are you saying the world should stop having children?"

"I couldn't do it."

"You'd be an amazing father."

"No. Don't say that." He sat up, cross-legged, and stared down at his feet. "I can't imagine you loving him."

Isaac scooted up so his back rested against the headboard. "He wasn't like this. I made him like this."

"So what was he like?"

Did Isaac even remember? His time in Charleston, his time before John, seemed like an alternate reality lived by someone else. The memories were movie clips that scrolled through his brain, pictures of a time that belonged to a stranger. He had been the stranger, his whole life, until he had met this deceptively strong creative writing teacher who taught him how easy it could be to love and laugh. But he had loved Simon, too, hadn't he? Hadn't he? "Simon was handsome and confident and smart. So very Charleston—the accent and the style. He charmed me right away. For a long time, we would only see each other in the afternoon. Meet in hotels, that sort of thing. Then, when Elizabeth would go on archaeological digs, I would stay at Simon's place. He would bring me breakfast in bed, these grits covered in butter."

John patted Isaac's tummy. "So you like men who cook."

"Obviously. But more than that, Simon showed me something. He was openly gay. Everyone knew, and no one cared. I'd never been in a relationship with someone like that before. Hell, I'd never even known someone like that, not with my upbringing."

"He showed you what was possible," John said.

"Yes, but I also always knew he had a temper. Our fights used to be brutal, especially about Elizabeth. He hated that I didn't love her anymore, but I stayed with her anyway. And the sex was..." He pressed fingers to his temple. "Looking back, I don't know if we were ever making love, John. I think we were just fucking."

John averted his gaze and plucked at the comforter. "Sometimes, you just need to fuck."

"Do I ever make love to you?"

John blushed. "Yeah."

"You can tell the difference?"

"Yes." He climbed onto Isaac's lap. "What's going to happen at dinner tonight?"

"I think I'm going to quit my job." He buried his face against John's chest.

"No." He tried pushing Isaac away but failed. "God, don't. I'm not worth it."

"Yes, you are," Isaac said against the soft fabric of his shirt.

"No, I—"

Isaac put his hand over John's mouth. "Stop it. I love you. Stop it."

John hid his face against the side of Isaac's neck. His stillness did not belie the fact that he cried.

STEPHEN'S WAS A block off Union. Isaac had never heard of the place because he and John never went on dates. They always ate at home, away from prying eyes. A bright, modern interior battled with the old-world scents of tomato and basil. Simon waited in a booth wearing a familiar navy-blue suit coat and shirt that had never looked so shabby.

A bottle of wine arrived as soon as Isaac sat. The waitress poured and smiled and talked about dinner specials when all Isaac could think about was running back to John, who he'd walked to campus in the rain earlier that day.

"Two plates of the pesto with chicken, please," Simon said.

Sure, fine. Isaac didn't want to eat but might as well get right to it.

Simon took a long sip of Cabernet.

"I'm quitting my job," Isaac said.

Simon nodded as if he'd expected as much. He might have been mad, but he wasn't stupid. "I understand what you see in him. He's strong. Much stronger than me."

"Don't sell yourself short."

"Is he okay?" Simon poked at the breadbasket.

"You scared him."

His jaw clenched and relaxed. "I really did just go over there to talk, maybe make him see what a horrible person you are. Instead, I was horrible. I really wanted to hurt him."

Thank God Isaac had arrived when he did. "If I quit my job, will you leave us alone?"

"You love him," Simon said. "I saw it that first day in the classroom—the way you ran to him when he was scared. I've never seen you like that, not even with me. We were never like that."

Isaac looked down and straightened his silverware. "Maybe I never thought you needed protecting."

"We all need protecting." Simon finished his wine and poured some more. "I think I was crazy to believe we'd work out. We'd been each other's dirty secret for so long, and the thing about secrets is they lose their power once they're told."

Isaac blinked away the burning in his eyes. "I'm so sorry, Simon."

Simon wouldn't look at him so instead observed the restaurant bar. "You seem happier here. More alive—which is messed up, considering this whole town is wearing a shadow. It's like you can feel it, feel something bad happened."

"Southern superstition rears its head."

"No. It's haunted here, and your sweetheart, I think he bears the brunt of it. You're going to lose him to that eventually, you know."

"To what?"

"The dark place." Simon put his napkin on his lap. "I always just wanted you to be happy, Isaac. I don't think that Yankee boy will make you happy forever, but I'm done with you. I've hurt enough, don't you think?"

Isaac folded his hands, a prayerful petition. "I'm sorry."

"You've said that. Maybe someday I'll believe you." He grabbed a piece of bread and nibbled the edge. "Will you tell John I didn't mean any harm?"

"I doubt he'll want to hear it."

Simon buttered the bread, methodically covering every edge, but didn't eat. "One thing I've learned through all this, Isaac? About love." He leaned his elbows on the table and looked like he might fall asleep or break down in tears. "The reality of love, it's not wonderful. It's living in fear every day of someone finding out what you really are."

Isaac left before the food arrived.

It took much longer than usual for Isaac to reach the crest of the hill where John's house waited, porch light lit. An unexpected weight clung to his back. Isaac opened the door without knocking and saw an obscure shape huddled against the foyer wall. The shape altered and moved until John emerged. Sitting a moment ago, he now stood, abandoning his whiskey glass on the tile floor.

Isaac turned on the light. Something about John in shadow—in that moment—actually frightened him.

"It's over," Isaac said.

The stricken look on John's face made Isaac rapidly reconsider his words.

"I mean, Simon's leaving. He's going. He knows I love you, and he's going. Our jobs are safe. You're safe."

"Are you sure?"

"He lost," Isaac said. "He doesn't like losing, but he knows how to gracefully accept defeat."

John hugged himself. "It wasn't a contest."

"No. I didn't mean that. He won't bother us again, though, I promise." He extended his hand. "Come here?"

John took quiet, shuffling steps forward until he could rest his cheek against Isaac's chest. He swallowed John's small frame in an aggressive embrace.

"Everything's all right now," he whispered into John's hair.

A puff of laughter displaced the quiet. "All right?" John's hands clung to the back of Isaac's coat like claws. He wondered if the fabric might tear.

Chapter Twelve

EARLY SATURDAY MORNING, Isaac rolled over in John's bed to find himself alone. The empty space at his side wasn't warm, even though Isaac's glowing cell phone read only 5:30 a.m. He sat up and listened, house quiet. From somewhere far away, he thought he heard the clunk of a coffee mug. He wrapped himself in an afghan and lumbered into the hall.

He smelled coffee immediately. A light was indeed on in the kitchen, but the unmistakable scent of sweet smoke floated from the direction of the front foyer. Hazily illuminated by dim office light, Isaac followed the cloud. As soon as he stepped inside, next to the bookcase, he shivered.

"John, it's freezing in here."

John's head popped up at the sound of Isaac's voice, curls bouncing. Isaac swept past and closed the open window, but it did not escape his notice that John slammed his laptop shut. Coffee and a half-smoked clove languished near his elbow.

"What are you doing?" Isaac asked.

"Uh..." John's entire face wrinkled up as he tried to hide a smile. "Watching porn?"

"You don't watch porn."

He leaned his elbows on the desk, folded his hands, and hid his mouth behind his fists.

"John?"

"Look, I didn't want to tell you yet, because it's early days." He leaned back in the expensive, aged leather chair Isaac knew was more comfortable than any furniture at Hambden. It had been John's since his time as a graduate student.

"Hey, Conlon. I don't play mind games before seven a.m."

John smiled up at him.

"Wait," Isaac said. "Are you writing again?"

"I...might be?"

Isaac tingled from his fingers to his toes. "Oh, my God!"

John spun the chair and stood. "No freaking out. I do not want you freaking out right now. It's only a couple chapters, and I don't know if it's any good."

"It'll be brilliant. You know it'll be brilliant." Isaac grabbed John's face and gave him a smooch. He'd already finished reading everything of John's—everything—every novel, short story, and academic treatise. Isaac had consumed every word, and with every word, he'd fallen more in love.

"You can't tell anyone."

"No." Isaac shook his head. "Okay."

"I don't want people to know yet." He turned away and paced to the window and back. "I don't know, it feels like too much pressure if people know I'm writing again. They'll want to know what it's about, and—"

Isaac's eyes widened.

"No. I don't talk about projects until they're done. I need my safe little creative vacuum."

"Yes. Sure."

John stared up at him and eventually laughed. "You look ridiculous."

"I'm sorry. I'm just really excited. Can I ask what brought this on? I know you haven't written since June. Is it the literary magazine, reading submissions?"

He shrugged, and they leaned against the desk, hip to hip. "Maybe." He cleared his throat. "Or maybe because I cut back on my meds recently."

"Oh. Your therapist's idea?"

"No."

"Oh." Isaac didn't want to say it, but he thought that might be bad. Isaac wasn't sure of the specific diagnosis, but John seemed to be doing well on the meds. He needed them, especially during panic attacks, so cutting back...

John nudged Isaac's arm. "Stop worrying. I just played with my dosage a little. Monday actually." He didn't say it but the day Simon showed up throwing fists. Isaac's face still wasn't completely healed.

Simon had left Lothos Thursday morning with nothing more than a final farewell text that Isaac had received while wrapped around a still-sleeping John. He was gone for good.

A big group had gone to dinner Thursday night to remember Demi's birthday, and although Janelle had gotten a bit drunk, she hadn't screamed at anyone. She and Anthony were back to playfully picking at each other.

Tommy and Isaac still weren't talking. Any camaraderie they'd once shared would have to be rebuilt. Isaac didn't blame him. How could he forgive someone who'd almost broken his best friend's heart? However, according to John, he'd argued a strong case in Isaac's defense—ironic since Simon was the lawyer. John had said something, had said enough, to keep Tommy from outright hating Isaac. It was a start at least.

"The drugs are good," John continued. "They help. I mean, I haven't had a nightmare in months. But I used to tell myself stories all the time. I'd be walking around campus, running dialogue or outlining scenes. It was how I'd put myself to sleep, too, the stories."

"Boring stories."

He shook his head. "No, it's just how my brain relaxes—by imagining things. I could erase the concerns of the day by disappearing into characters that weren't me, conflicts that weren't mine. Then, after the shooting, I could only see that day in June, over and over. The curse of a vivid imagination." He reached for the clove cigarette that had burned out and used a match to relight it. He took a long inhale and blew smoke toward the ceiling. "Hence, the drugs."

"What are the drugs for exactly? PTSD?"

"Mm-hmm." He tapped the clove on the ashtray. "For a while there, I couldn't leave the house. Like, at all. You know I still have episodes. I'm not good with loud noises or big crowds. Sometimes, I swear I hear Chris's voice on College Green. It's fucked up."

Isaac rested a hand over his. "I can't imagine how hard it was for you to come back here."

He shrugged. "I couldn't hide forever."

"Thank God." He gave John's hand a squeeze. "I want to know about this stuff. Your mental health. Is that okay? You'll let me know if you're having a bad day?"

John nodded and stubbed out his smoke.

"I can't believe you didn't tell me you were writing again."

John stood and opened the window, waving smoke out into the late October cold. "I knew you'd fanboy, and what if this is just a fluke? What if I'm permanently broken?" He put on a fantastic horror movie face, hands to his cheeks. "What if I'm nothing more than a college professor for the rest of my life?"

Isaac chuckled. "Shut it."

"Teaching comp to business majors. Oh, my God!" Laughing, he leaned his chest on Isaac's and melted. Isaac had to wrap his arms around him to keep him from sliding to the floor. "You should go back to bed." He spoke against Isaac's blanketed body.

"Only if you promise to write some more."

"Deal."

"But it seriously is an icebox in here." He tilted them both to standing and wrapped the big afghan around John's shoulders. "Take this."

John pulled the fabric over his head like a babushka, grasped it tightly under his chin, and yawned. "What time is Cleo's Halloween party?"

"Seven."

"I'll nap this afternoon." He circled the desk and sat, embraced by his blanket. After he opened his computer, he glared up at Isaac—the ire of which was greatly dwindled by his resemblance to a small Russian woman. "If you even try to sneak a peek, I will cut you off from sex for...two days."

Isaac scoffed. "You can't last that long."

"Don't test me."

He rolled his eyes—a habit he'd picked up from John—and shivered as he walked back through the house in nothing but boxers. He shimmied under the warm covers and pulled them up to his chin before falling into a blessedly dreamless sleep.

CLEO LIVED IN a little one-story house up a different hill than John. Isaac had to pass about three million costumed college students—and their visiting friends—on the way up there. Apparently, unbeknownst to Isaac, Hambden University was famous for its Halloween party, overshadowed by only Wisconsin, John's alma mater. All of Union Street closed down for a massive street party that would soon be underway, which meant Isaac was definitely sleeping at John's. The ruckus downtown might never end.

Cleo being Cleo had decorated her porch with purple lights. A couple homemade tombstones built a tiny cemetery in the front yard. "The Time Warp" played on the stereo inside, where Isaac had earlier greeted some of his coworkers while politely ignoring everyone else. He wasn't there to mingle but to make Cleo happy. The hostess was dressed as a witch. Well, she wore a witch's hat, at least. It wasn't a costume party—more a celebration of a spooky night in which all of Lothos drowned under the combined weight of tourists, alcohol, and childish pranks. Speaking of, a university-wide email had gone out earlier that week: no one was to dress like Chris Frank. Anyone who did would be arrested and expelled.

Isaac and Tommy stood silently against the wall with pumpkin beers, watching a few people dance in the living room—a living room covered in vintage movie posters. Although the party music played from a stereo, Cleo's turntable sat where a TV might be, and a massive vinyl collection took the place of books.

John had been gone for a while, Cleo having kidnapped him and taken him to her bedroom—which might have been scandalous if it were anyone else. Instead, it was just John and Cleo, Cleo and John.

Tommy, although standing right next to Isaac, had yet to say a word until…

"This is the one night of the year when I feel like a dirty, old man," Tommy said.

"Sorry?"

"Later, John will drag us down the hill to Union Street because he likes seeing all the costumes, and I hate running into students dressed as slutty…cats, or whatever. It's 'slutty' everything down there, I swear, and it makes me feel like a filthy, old man." He shook his head and took another sip of beer.

A couple started dancing—for real—around the center of the floor, because of course they did. Of course, Cleo's friends would know how to ballroom dance. Maybe she'd met them when she and John had taken classes of their own.

"Huh," Isaac said. "Wonder what my equivalent would be to slutty cats."

Tommy pushed his glasses farther up his nose. "A guy dressed like Freddie Mercury?" He pulled on the collar of his shirt. "I'm still pissed at you. So you know."

"I deserve that."

"Yeah, you fucking do." He lowered his voice, which made Isaac lean closer to hear over the music. "John put in a good word, said you treat him right. Except for the whole ex-boyfriend bullshit."

"I'm really sorry, Tommy."

"Yes. You are. But maybe we can be friends again, eventually, all right? Just give me time." He held up his beer, and Isaac clinked his against it immediately.

John moonwalked out of the kitchen, spun, and presented jazz hands. His big, green eyes were always soulful, but now, the effect was greatly intensified by smoky makeup. His cheekbones shimmered.

"Jesus," Isaac whispered. Every atom in his body directed him to toss John over his shoulder, carry him home, and tear him to shreds.

"He finally let me do his makeup!" Cleo crooned. "Just look at his eyelashes!"

Tommy smirked. "Of course you could pull off women's makeup."

"Want some?" John asked. He made kissy faces at Tommy until Tommy laughed and literally shoved him away by the face.

"Don't touch my masterpiece!" Cleo said. She handed John a red Solo cup filled with what she'd earlier called "Hairy Buffalo"—some deadly mix of grain alcohol, punch, and fruit—and disappeared back the way she'd come.

John eyed the room. Under a flannel button-down, he wore a T-shirt that read, *This is my Halloween T-shirt.* "So did anyone do anything drunk and embarrassing yet?"

"Well, you do have makeup on," Tommy said.

"Come on, man, she's been begging to do that for years."

Tommy yelled at Isaac over the music. "Apparently, he has 'perfect bone structure.'" Both John and Tommy made the shape of quotations marks with their fingers at the same time.

A purple-haired woman in a gothic baby-doll dress shimmied into their conversation and grabbed Tommy by the hand. "Come on, four-eyes, dance with me!"

Tommy didn't fight her one bit.

John nudged Isaac with his elbow. "You like the makeup."

He hoped his pants didn't show how much. He leaned a little closer to be heard by John but no one else. "What have you done to me? You've made lung cancer hot, and now this? Cleo's right about the eyelashes; when you blink, I feel a breeze."

"Well, I promise you can mess it all up later."

"I am going to fuck the hell out of you later."

John coughed on his drink.

Cleo bopped up next to them. "Come on, John, let's dance!" She grabbed his cup and chugged.

People made room. Tommy did his best to keep up with the purple-haired lady while Cleo and John floated and spun like ballroom champs. It was amazing that such a lanky guy could be so graceful, but he knew all the steps, and he was a strong lead. Where he led, Cleo followed. He said something that made her laugh, and she leaned her face right against his neck, her hand sliding down around his waist.

Cleo loved John. Isaac wasn't sure in what way, but it was obvious in how she touched him and sought his attentions. Theirs was a friendship, obviously, but Isaac wondered if Cleo secretly yearned for what she couldn't have.

When an old swing standard started up, half the room cheered. Yes, these were Cleo's people—but maybe they could be Isaac's too? He didn't know how to dance, but...

He walked up to John and Cleo, midstep. For a second, he almost asked Cleo if he could cut in and mentally slapped himself. Instead, he asked John, thank goodness.

"But I don't know how to dance," he clarified. "Cleo, I was wondering if you could show me?"

John beamed up at him, and Cleo clapped her hands. "Yes! I would love to!"

Isaac tried to listen, focus, and not step on her toes, but John stood right there, smiling with his eyeliner and flashy cheekbones. He wanted to have John's hand in his and John's voice in his ear counting the steps.

The unfamiliar need to make a lovesick pronouncement rattled Isaac's spine, and it wasn't the first time. Just that morning, after he'd gone back to sleep, when John had roused him at eight with his famous coffee—looking all writing ruffled and brilliant—Isaac had wanted to open the front door and shout down the hill, "This man! Do you see him? He's beautiful and amazing and brave, and he's all mine!"

He hadn't, of course, shouted. Instead, he'd wrestled John under the covers for an early morning make out. He'd swallowed John's protests of "But your coffee will get cold," with open-mouthed kisses, until John had melted into a soft, warm puddle of want.

Cleo chirped when he stepped on her high-heeled foot.

"Sorry! Sorry."

"You're getting better." She smiled. "Just need to relax your shoulders. You look like Lurch from *The Addams Family*."

John guffawed and walked over to Tommy, who'd taken a break in his own mad dancing to get another beer. When the next song had a salsa beat, Isaac pled ignorance and skulked toward the kitchen where he poured himself a single cup of "Hairy Buffalo" and realized how dangerous it probably was since he couldn't taste a bit of booze.

An hour later, his head light, he followed the rest of the party down the hill into the heart of Lothos. Union Street had been transformed. Usually all brick roads and buildings, it was now a living, moving mass of merriment, decorated in orange twinkle lights and flickering jack-o'-lanterns. The air smelled of wet leaves and clove, especially as John and Cleo split a smoke on the walk down. Once they prepared to enter the melee, John slowed down and walked next to Isaac, their fingertips just barely brushing.

Immediately, Isaac understood what Tommy had been talking about. Anything could be "slutty," even a police uniform, apparently. There were actual cops there, too, observing the crowd, probably watching for open containers. It had to be the Lothos jail's busiest night of the year.

John apparently wasn't interested in the slutty stuff. When he saw a bloody Pennywise on stilts, he grabbed Isaac's hand and pointed. He actually squeaked when an impressive Edward Scissorhands ambled by. Isaac watched him, grinning so hard it almost hurt. So this was John, wide-eyed with wonder, looking like a giddy teenager on Union Street. This was John without the memory of Chris Frank—without the darkness that sometimes curled his shoulders forward and crinkled his eyes. John before June.

"Oh, my God, I found Waldo!" He pointed to a guy in a striped shirt.

Isaac laughed and tried not to pick John up and swing him around.

AFTER AN HOUR in downtown Lothos spent costume spotting, they all went back to Cleo's. The bars were too packed to get inside, so drinking continued at her place until guests started making excuses. John and Isaac were careful to leave separately.

Isaac waited in John's darkened foyer right by the front door, so when it slowly opened, he ducked behind to hide. Although the worst at hide-and-seek his entire life, even someone of Isaac's height could find solace in shadow. When John crossed the threshold—and before he could even touch the lock—Isaac wrapped him in a bear hug from behind that made John startle and yelp. He gripped Isaac's hands hard. "Shit, you scared me."

"Well, it is Halloween. Maybe your house is haunted." He made ghostly vowel sounds before spinning John around and pinning him to the wall with his hips.

In makeup, in the dark, John resembled a gorgeous ghoul. He stared up at Isaac from below eyelashes thick with mascara. "And what kind of spirit would you be? Maybe a big, buff Roman gladiator?"

He tilted John's chin up. "Want to be my helpless slave boy?"

John snickered. "I'm never helpless."

"No." He leaned down and sucked John's earlobe. "That's true." His hand snaked down John's stomach and right into the front of his jeans.

John gripped Isaac's elbows and sighed.

John wasn't helpless, no, but he was a pliant, submissive lover whose ever-clasping hands denoted his need to be cared for, engulfed. Sometimes, he fucked in a way that made Isaac feel as though he consumed John— as if John wanted to be absorbed and erased into Isaac's skin.

With no resistance, John allowed himself to be carried into the office and bent over the desk's edge in memory of, or maybe in homage to, the writing he'd done that morning, words Isaac couldn't wait to devour. He would, for now, devour the writer instead.

After making sure John was comfortable with his made-up face pressed to the desktop, Isaac pulled John's jeans down over his slim hips and *tsked*. "Really?"

"What?" John asked, innocent as ever.

"No underwear." He knelt behind John, and before John could make a snappy retort, Isaac spread his cheeks and licked into him.

"Oh!"

They hadn't done that before, even if Isaac had wanted to. He hadn't even thought to ask if it was something John wanted, so he pulled back and said, "Is this okay?"

John's forehead smacked into the table twice. "Yes. Yes, please."

Isaac continued his ministrations. He didn't take pause until he noticed John's thighs trembled, and he didn't seem to be breathing. "John? You with me?"

"Fuck. Yeah, I'm going to come."

Isaac, still on his knees, massaged John's ass and gave a teasing kiss to each cheek. "I can't wait to feel you on my tongue."

Thirty seconds of deep licks later, John, usually so quiet in his orgasms, came with a resonant cry that arched his chest off the desk. Isaac stood slowly and wiped his face on the back of John's shirt before kissing his neck.

John kept his face hidden against the desk. "Sorry. Wow, no one's done that in a while."

"What are you sorry for?" He leaned his front against John's back. "That was incredible."

John shimmied slightly, enough to wedge Isaac's clothed erection right against his cleft. "Need you." Even bent over and basically blind to his surroundings, he found the wherewithal to open the nearest desk drawer and pull out a condom.

"Do you keep condoms all over the house?"

A small smile flowered on his face, although he seemed to be drifting—either on sex or sleep.

Their fuck was slow and deep like a calm ocean undertow. John's hands held to either side of the desk as Isaac rocked into him, deeper with every thrust until he basically remained fully seated, doing nothing more than moving his hips in small circles.

John cursed suddenly, and Isaac froze. "Am I hurting you?"

"There is no way I'm going to come again." It wasn't a statement of surety but a statement of awe.

Isaac reached below John where his hips pressed against the desk and found him hard. "Holy shit, yes, you are."

He continued with the slow, deep tease. One of John's hands flailed back, and his fingers curled in the short hair at Isaac's nape. For a better grip, Isaac took hold of John's waist, and his fingers almost touched, so small the frame of his panting lover. He could break him if he wanted.

"Harder."

Isaac acquiesced.

"Hard—oh, fuck, right there. Right..." John's deep voice crackled like static as his body clenched around Isaac. This time, John came silently.

Isaac felt his own orgasm down to his toes. With numb lips, he kissed at John's curled shoulders and rubbed his nose behind his ear. "I love you."

John, drunk on alcohol and endorphins, replied, "I don't know why."

HE HOPED A shower would help his hangover. Leaving a naked, makeup-covered John in bed, Isaac turned the water to scald and stepped beneath the merciless spray. Isaac rubbed John's shampoo into his scalp—some outrageously expensive stuff that made his chocolate-brown hair shine like silk. Isaac gargled shower water and spit. He leaned his hands on the shower walls and let the water tumble over his shoulders and down his back.

"I don't know why."

In moments like that, Isaac wanted to shake John, but he'd let it go to retain the memory of a perfect night. He'd fallen asleep, only to be woken again later with John riding him, makeup a melted mess like a watercolor left in the rain.

He turned off the shower. Towel around his waist, he returned to the bedroom to find John awake and blinking up at him. "How scary do I look right now?"

"Well, that pillowcase might be ruined."

He stretched, and the sheet slid, revealing the V of his hips. "Did you have fun last night?"

"Before or after we got home?"

John smiled. "Both?"

Isaac stood above him. "I had a very good time last night."

John opened his mouth, and then closed it. He stared at the ceiling and bit his bottom lip, provoking a Pavlovian response that made Isaac clutch tighter to his towel.

"John, what is it?"

He traced a nonexistent pattern on the blankets. "What we have is really intense. Don't you think?"

"I don't know." He did know. He knew exactly. Why was he lying?

"It scares you sometimes, what we have. I see it when you look at me and look away. You love me, but it's more. You reach for me like you think I'm going to disappear."

Isaac shrugged and removed the towel to dry his hair. "Everything else good has." It was a statement of fact, not a request for pity.

John just nodded.

Isaac tossed the towel, sat, and touched John's cheek. "Okay, I do love you, and it is intense, and I am scared."

John smirked. "There. Was that so hard?"

"Yeah. It was. Now, go wash your face because you do, in fact, look like a horror movie character."

He buried his cheek against the stained pillowcase. "Hey, it's Halloween."

"Not anymore. Let's order pizza today and watch football."

John sighed. "Fuck, I just got hard again."

Isaac snorted and pulled his pajamas from the "Isaac drawer." He made their coffee that morning, but it wasn't nearly as good as John's.

Chapter Thirteen

IN A STRIPED shirt and blazer, John leaned against the classroom's front desk and crossed his arms. All staff members of *Being Frank* waited silently, even Janelle and Anthony, because they knew John was not one for standing in front of the class, lecturing. With the exuberance of a hormonal teen, he usually walked up and down rows, throwing out ideas until students picked up the thread. Not today apparently—and there was the matter of the vote. Isaac stood off to the side against a wall, giving John space.

"I'd like to apologize for my behavior last week," he said. "I was completely unprofessional. I let these yahoos—" Janelle and Anthony ducked their heads. "—get a little out of hand. I know a bad day is no excuse, but I was having a really bad day."

Janelle frowned. "Are you feeling better now?"

"Yeah, I'm fine. But we have more important business to deal with." He paused for a long, slow breath. "We all have access to the shared documents in Google Docs, so we've all been able to read some of the submissions. So far, we've received a lot of submissions that suck, but it's very early. I have no doubt this could be the coolest thing we've ever done in the English Department—bravest thing, at least. However, as we so vocally debated last Tuesday, there's an issue of politics. Agenda." He crossed his ankles, imitating a nervous human pretzel. "Do you want my opinion, or do you just want to vote?"

"We want to hear what you think, man," Anthony said.

John's eyes flickered just once to Isaac. "Every piece we receive is going to have an opinion, either intentional or not. That's the blessing and curse of this medium. We put a little of ourselves into everything we write, agreed?"

A crowd of nods.

"We have to be open to…everyone." He sighed. "Liberal, conservative, Christian, atheist. Anger, sadness, love, hate; I don't feel right censoring any of that. But the format is another issue entirely, okay? The essay that brought about this discussion is academic in nature, no matter how well written the argument. I don't feel comfortable making *Being Frank* a platform for debate; we have a newspaper for that. I want this to be a safe space for students to express their emotions. They might not feel safe out there." He pointed to the window, to College Green. "But maybe they can feel safe on the page. Does that make sense?"

Janelle nodded. "You're right, John. That essay has no place in a literary magazine. I was wrong last week."

"Wait." Anthony dug around in his bag. "I need to get my phone to record. Can you say that again slowly? The part about you being wrong?"

She rolled her eyes, and Isaac hid a smile behind his hand.

"This isn't up to Janelle and me," John said. "I want to hear from all of you. I want to hear what you think about this."

A girl with glasses and a ponytail raised her hand. "We can't judge. Quality, yes, but content?" She shook her head. "We have to keep a distance."

"Very good. Yes." John gripped the desk and looked at his feet. "I think we have to keep a distance in general. For the next few months, we're going to be reading repeatedly about what happened in June. I haven't recovered yet; I don't know if you have. If you need to step away, step away. If there's something that really bothers you..." He snapped his fingers. "Look, okay, we'll create a system. Like a checklist. If a submission hits you too hard, pass it on. Someone else can read it."

"If it hits us hard, isn't that the point?" Janelle asked.

"Hitting hard and hitting *too* hard are different things," Isaac added. He was beginning to feel like a creeper, lurking against the wall.

"I'm not a child," she said.

John clicked his tongue. "Yes, you are. I know you all went through something you didn't deserve, but don't be callous. Don't bury what happened. Feel it. Put it on the page. Don't put on a tough front, not for me." He eyed each of them in turn. "We decided to do something radical with the literary magazine this year. Radical is never easy. The deeper we go, the harder things are going to get. The more phone calls from parents I'm going to have to deal with and angry students and angry faculty. But if this is what we want to do—give voices to the grieving and the dead—I will fight for you." His voice lost its power. "As much as I can."

"Me too," Isaac said.

John smiled. "See? And no one's going to mess with Isaac because he's a giant. Does anyone else have anything they'd like to say?"

No one answered.

John raised his right hand. "Opinion-based treatise." He raised his left. "Or fearless emotional truth."

Every left hand rose. Fearless they would be.

ISAAC WALKED UP the nighttime steps of Ellis Hall. On the third floor, he knocked on every door, but all were locked. The building was quiet because it was night, and no one hung around there at night. Candles flared to light, illuminating flowers and faces of the dead—a makeshift altar in the hall that belonged on College Green. He knelt when he recognized a picture of John, "RIP" written across his forehead. Blood poured from the base of his neck where the bullet would have been if Chris had pulled the trigger. But he hadn't; John was alive.

Where was John?

Isaac hurried back down the candlelit hall and tried to go the way he'd come, but the door to the stairs was now locked too. He banged on it—*bang, bang, bang.*

He kept knocking until the noise woke him, and he realized someone was actually knocking on his front door. Rolling over in bed, he groaned and grabbed his glowing cell: 3:00 a.m.

"What the..." In nothing but boxers, he grabbed a shirt and pulled it over his head. "Who is it?"

"Freddy Krueger."

Isaac opened the front door, lock fixed after Simon's departure. "What are you doing here?"

John leaned forward and back on his toes, hands in his jeans pockets. Eyes wide, he looked like he'd had too much coffee. "Couldn't sleep."

"So now I can't sleep."

"Yeah." John walked in and headed for the kitchen.

Isaac winced from the sudden white light while John opened and closed cabinets.

"Where's my whiskey?"

"Shit." Isaac wiped the sleep from his eyes and remembered that horrible night with Simon.

"You drank all my whiskey?" John kicked a cupboard closed. "Dick."

"I owe you a bottle."

John walked back in and did a face-plant onto the couch, gangly legs hanging over the arm.

Isaac crouched next to his face. "What's going on?"

John grumbled against the couch cushion. "I had a bad dream."

"I didn't think you dreamed at all." He sat on the floor, the better to touch John's hair, still cold with November chill. "Maybe going off your meds isn't a good idea."

"I told you I'm not going off them. Just cutting back."

"Well?"

He shifted onto his back with a huff. "I can't write on the drugs. They're not good for me, and I hate them."

"But you need them."

John leaned up and crackled his knuckles. Where was all this energy coming from? "You know, one fucked-up thing happens in your life, and your brain just..." He put his hands by his head and mimicked the sound of an explosion. "You know that thing I told them tonight about keeping a distance from the work? That was for me. Reading all this shit, Isaac, seeing that day from all these different perspectives? It's like playing it on repeat from different camera angles."

"Do you want to stop?"

"No." His voice sounded hoarse. "No, it's just me. Dutifully carrying around my residual guilt."

Isaac joined him on the couch. "You have nothing to be guilty about."

John laughed, and the sound sent a shiver down Isaac's spine.

"I hate when you laugh like that," he said. "It's awful."

"Well, sometimes, I'm awful." And John looked it—exhausted but awake, fingers twitching against his knees like he hid insects in his skin.

"That's not what I meant."

He scratched his nose. His darting eyes studied the room but didn't seem to focus on anything. "Let's fuck."

Isaac coasted his hand up and down John's back. "I don't think that's a good idea right now."

"Maybe Adam would be up for quickie."

"Fuck, John." Isaac stood and circled the coffee table. "Why the hell are you mad at me?"

He pulled his hair. "I need you to take me apart right now and put me back together with better parts."

"I love all your parts."

"Not...this." He hugged himself. "Whatever this is."

"John, I'm out of my depth here. I don't know what to say or do to make this better. I wish I knew. Maybe you should see your therapist tomorrow."

"No, I don't want to talk about it. Talk, talk." He squeezed his eyes shut and rubbed his forehead. "Please just take me to bed. And not for sleeping. I don't want to sleep anymore."

Isaac didn't move any closer. He kept his distance because he thought touching John might break them both. "What did you dream about tonight?"

John held himself tighter and rocked forward and back. "Everyone was dead. Except for me. Why was I still alive?"

Isaac sat on the coffee table and grabbed John by the shoulders. He stopped the rocking, but it took a minute for John to look up. He was used to feeling John's gaze, but in that moment, he remembered the first time they'd met—the way that, despite Isaac's greater height, John had somehow made him feel small with just a look. It was the bottomless nature of those eyes, those drowning pools of green, emotive enough to transfer despair, confusion, and fear, like a frigid wind to the face.

"I don't know why, John, but you are. You're still alive."

"Prove it," he said. He stood, took Isaac's hand, and dragged him to the bedroom.

ISAAC'S ALARM AT seven might as well have been a damn rooster in his tiny bedroom. He cussed and clawed for his cell phone only to be met by a news alert received at five a.m. John, blessedly, still dozed behind him, wedged between Isaac and the wall in his twin bed. It was a good thing John was so thin, or they never would have fit.

Quietly, Isaac climbed out of bed and went to the living room. He turned on the TV and kept the volume on mute as he scrolled through a couple news stations, eventually settling on one, and turned up the volume a bit. Words scrolled across the screen above a backdrop of police light in the Miami night.

Forty-nine killed in gay club. Shooter has suspected terrorist ties.

He pressed his lips together—hard—as his eyes burned.

No, not this, not another one. It was getting worse and fast. Isaac glanced toward his front window, dread curling his hands into fists, as if he could feel *them*—the would-be shooters, the kids waiting to go crazy. But there were too many. They were everywhere.

A pretty newscaster with a fake tan spoke softly. "Gunfire was first reported at one thirty in the morning at Metro nightclub, although the standoff continued for three hours with over two hundred hostages trapped inside. The police aren't sure—"

Isaac turned off the TV as soon as he heard John behind him.

Hair askew, he snarled, "Don't you dare turn that off." He snatched the remote and turned the TV back on, volume up. Side by side, they watched the carnage, the screaming, the 911 recordings, and dead bodies under sheets. "Is that Miami?"

"Yeah."

John dropped the remote. "Oh, my God. Where's my phone?"

"Your phone?"

"My phone!" He ran back to the bedroom, where Isaac heard the telltale sound of clothes being thrown about.

Isaac moved to follow, but before he could cross the threshold into his room, John smacked into his chest coming back out. His phone went flying. He cussed and chased it, scooping it up in shaking hands.

"John? What—"

He dialed and held the phone to his ear. "Pick up. Pick up, you son of a bitch. Don't be dead." John's eyes never left the TV.

Isaac took a step away. John must know someone in Miami—probably a gay someone, a someone who frequented bars like Metro—so Isaac, despite his ignorance, repeated *Don't be dead* in his own head.

The volume was up so loud on John's phone, Isaac heard an unfamiliar male voice answer on the line, followed by John's panicked voice. "Ben, are you okay?"

"Yeah, we didn't go out last night."

Isaac's own phone buzzed in his hand with a text from Tommy. *Don't let John watch the news.*

"Christ." John leaned his forehead against the nearest doorframe. "Did you...is everyone all right? I mean..."

"We don't know yet, sweetie." Ben, whoever Ben was, used pet names? "Everyone's calling everyone, and people aren't picking up, and the cops aren't releasing anything. It's a mess."

John knocked his forehead into the door once. "That's what you get for moving to Florida."

Ben's exhale crackled the connection. "I miss you."

"Miss you too. Call me later?"

They hung up. John poked at a drip of thick, dried paint—evidence of a cheap job. "Ben's a friend of mine from college. He moved to Florida after graduation. He didn't like the cold."

Now, Isaac remembered. "I thought he was your boyfriend in college."

John shrugged. "As much as I did boyfriends back then, I guess." He turned and slid down the wall to sit just as his phone vibrated. He lifted the screen. "Christ, it's my mom. Maman? *Oui, je sais.*"

Isaac didn't understand the rest of it, but it sounded at first quiet, then louder, then faster.

He texted Tommy. *He already knows.*

Shit.

John's French flowed like a fountain, alternating between tense to sad to soft to back again. Isaac was beginning to suspect John's relationship with his European mother resembled a volcano—very warm but prone to explosion—further demonstrated when John hung up the phone suddenly and threw it across the room.

"She wants me home in Wisconsin."

"Because of Ben?"

"What? No. She says nothing feels safe." He stood and tugged his fingers through his hair, getting it out of his face just as Isaac saw the time.

He spoke slowly, hating every word. "I need to get ready for class."

"Fine. Can I stay here today?"

"John—"

"I could have Cleo bring my computer and school work from my house on her way to campus, drop them here."

"Jesus, John, she can't know you're here. She can't know about us at all."

John covered his mouth. "Shit, I'm sorry. I don't know what I was thinking."

And that was worrisome. John knew the rules of their relationship. Their covert behaviors were second nature by then. If John was rattled enough to forget the furtive nature of their affair, what else might he forget? What else might he let slide? If Isaac asked him to tell him the truth, the whole truth, about June 6 on College Green right that very moment, he probably would.

John studied the sun-soaked curtains. "I don't want to go out there."

"Look, I understand. Come here." Isaac grabbed him by the wrist and pulled him close. "But we can't do this, John. Every time something bad happens, we can't hide in our houses, because lots of bad things are happening. You can't shut down every time some madman shoots up a bar or a school, or you'll be shutting down every day."

"I can't believe we have to say that."

Like ripping off a Band-Aid, Isaac said, "I want you to keep taking your meds."

John pushed his hands away. "I *am* taking them. I'm just cutting back."

"I don't want you to cut back."

John stood. "Well, that's nice, but it's not your fucking decision." He brushed more hair from his face, but it was like he had fidgeting follicles. They tumbled back and shaded his eyes. "I'm going home."

"Let me shower. I'll walk you."

"No." He disappeared back into the bedroom and stumbled out, tugging on his clothes. "I'll be fine. What's the worst that can happen?" He smiled in the fake way that made Isaac's stomach churn.

"You don't look okay."

"I'm fine. Hey, Wisconsin's playing this Saturday night. Big Ten game. Was thinking of watching it with the boys at Joe's Pub. Do you want to go?"

"You're changing the subject."

John held his hands up and grinned. "There's nothing else to talk about. A bunch of gay kids got shot in Miami last night, and my friend is fine, and we have to work, so..." He kissed Isaac on the cheek.

Isaac grabbed him by the upper arm before he could dash. "Love you."

He studied Isaac's lips. "I know." Outside the front door, his light footsteps danced down Isaac's steps.

Isaac texted Tommy. *Keep an eye on John today.*

Is he okay?

I don't think so.

He should have told Tommy about the drugs, about how John was dreaming again—about how in bed last night, he'd clutched and clawed, and once, tried to hide his crying. But maybe that was too intimate. It felt too intimate. No mystery, John had secrets. If John wanted to share things with Tommy, he would. They were best friends, after all. Isaac was just the boyfriend.

CLEO SANG AT Crocodile Lounge that night, so attendance was more mandatory than suggested. Isaac knew John loved hearing her sing; maybe it would make him feel better. When Isaac arrived after a late class, the show was in full swing, as was the bar and dance floor, packed with people. Cleo wore a gauzy, baby-blue dress and bright-red beehive. She waved from the stage and sang "Blue Moon."

John and Tommy shouted at him from the bar, glowing in shades of red and purple from the overhead mood lights. Known for its Creole food, the place smelled like butter and spicy sausage. Isaac itched his nose to prevent a sneeze.

John gave him a quick hug, which was a definite no-no. They didn't touch much in public. Isaac took a hurried step back, almost pulling John with him, but no one seemed to notice.

"Good day?" John smiled.

"Sure. You?"

He shrugged and did a little dance step closer to the stage, closer to Cleo.

"What do you want to drink, Isaac?" Tommy nodded to the bar and kept nodding—a silent prompt to come closer.

"I'm good, thanks." Isaac whispered, "How does he seem to you?"

"Honestly? Great. What did you say to him this morning?"

Isaac tried to think of one thing in particular, but his day was muddled with memories of lectures and poorly written papers. "I guess I said a lot of things."

Tommy shook his head and downed a shot of something gold. "Well, keep saying them. Or keep having *the sex*. Whatever. He hasn't been like this since before, you know, murder."

Isaac knew his face was wrinkling and didn't care. "Are you sure?"

"Seriously. He seems lighter. And, well, drunk, but we always used to get drunk together before he went away for the summer. He's been a lot more subdued socially since June. This is..." Tommy grinned so big, the room lit up. "He's back, man." He clasped Isaac on the shoulder just as John came sprinting toward them.

"Cleo wants a shot of honey whiskey for her throat!" Although he'd barely lifted his voice above the crowd noise, the bartender rushed over and poured a shot without question. John, the dutiful assistant, took it back to the stage but didn't abandon his post without bowing to the blushing songstress twice.

"He said he talked to Ben earlier," Tommy said. "So maybe that's helping too."

"They're close? He hasn't mentioned him much."

"They were really close when they were younger, but they still keep in touch. I mean, Ben was, you know." He glanced up at Isaac and immediately took a sip of his drink. "Or maybe you don't know. Ben's the only guy John ever loved. Dropped the L-word. Hasn't happened since."

Isaac felt the room tilt as he realized how desperate he was to hear that very word from John. He struggled for some sense of levity. After all, he was in a great bar listening to great music standing next to a great friend while watching, possibly, the greatest thing that had ever happened to him—and all Isaac could feel was an ache in his chest.

"Maybe I'll have one drink."

"My man." Tommy smacked him on the back. At least things were back to normal between them, despite the Simon disaster.

Isaac ordered a whiskey-scotch blend with a couple ice cubes and almost choked on a sip when John skidded to his side. "Hey, Cleo's asking for requests. You want to hear anything?"

"We don't have a song, do we?"

John pressed his lips together until they wrinkled. "Damn. Guess not."

"You seem to be feeling better."

"That's because I heard you this morning." He jumped when a full beer slid right at him from down the bar. A little liquid sloshed over the top as he glared at a smiling, toasting Tommy. "You told me I couldn't let every shooting affect me. They're happening constantly. It's the new fucking normal."

"John—"

"No. Listen. I'm alive. I need to start acting like it."

He allowed himself a single touch—a poke to John's forearm. "You've always felt very alive to me."

"Well, hold on to your hat, cowboy."

"John!" Cleo's voice, loud on a good day, echoed through the microphone. "Song request?"

"Uh..." He looked at Isaac and looked some more. "How about 'Smile,' by Charlie Chaplin?"

Cleo winked before conversing with the band.

When the music started soft and slow, John leaned close and hummed along—until Tommy handed him a shot and dragged him to the crowded dance floor to chat up some young ladies who had to be grad students. Although Tommy wasn't the best-looking guy, he made them laugh almost immediately while John smiled and existed. The women listened to Tommy, but their eyes kept going to John. Maybe they knew him as the "Hambden hero" or maybe they were wondering how a Botticelli angel escaped a fresco.

Isaac wouldn't have stayed so late, but he worried about John and his ambitious alcohol consumption—so he stayed until the final set ended and Cleo bowed to a clapping crowd. Canned jazz music replaced the live band, and John took one turn around the floor with Cleo before seeking Isaac.

"I'm going home," he said.

"I'll walk you."

John yawned and started walking as if this was the expected outcome. His eyelids floated at half-mast, and he wore a constant close-lipped smile. Once outside, they simultaneously shoved hands in pockets.

Isaac shivered. "I need to buy you gloves."

John walked quickly up the sidewalk—as quick as he could, veering slightly left and right with every step. "I have so many gloves. I need to buy *you* gloves."

"Don't have a pair to loan me?"

John giggled and almost fell off a curb. "My gloves would fit your, like, pinky."

"Fair enough."

Away from the gentle glow of downtown Lothos, they walked closer, arms brushing with every step. A block up the hill, Isaac slung his arm around John's shoulder and kissed the side of his head. John hummed his pleasure. Two blocks up and close to John's house, Isaac offered his back. John jumped on without question, arms around Isaac's neck as he rode him up the driveway.

Isaac didn't even pause in the foyer. He carried John to the bedroom and tossed him lightly on the unmade mess of blankets and pillows. He huffed when his back hit the bed and immediately rolled onto his stomach, burying his head in a pillow.

"The room...is spinning," John said.

"How bad?"

"Umm..."

When he didn't respond, Isaac realized he'd passed out. He leaned forward to check. Yes, eyes shut, lips parted, breathing in gentle puffs. Isaac hurried to the bathroom and opened the medicine cabinet. There it was, the Prazosin. He grabbed a pill and glass of water before doing a light jog to John's bedroom.

He rested his hand on John's shoulder and shook.

"Mm?"

"You need to take your pill," Isaac said.

John's right eye cracked open before he leaned up on one elbow and took the proffered goods. Pill swallowed, his head crashed back to the pillow. "If you want to hump some part of my body, you can. Just don't wake me up."

"It'd be like having sex with a corpse."

"A warm corpse, though."

Isaac twirled a piece of John's hair between his fingers. "I'll pass."

"Mm..." And he was out again.

Isaac watched him for a while—this unexpected, delicate creature he was allowed to touch. He remembered saying it once; he hadn't thought John would be a problem for him. Historically, he'd wanted manly men—men his own size and strength. Perhaps, he'd been trying to get as far away from Elizabeth as possible in that respect. And then along came John Conlon.

Isaac could fit both his wrists in one hand. He bruised too easily. Kissing his mouth was like kissing an exotic, rare fruit, and he rarely needed to shave. A Disney princess would scalp him for his hair, yet there was the surprisingly deep voice, the huge feet, and those thick eyebrows that screamed *man.* There was the way they sometimes wrestled during sex like two teenage boys, laughing until the laughter was replaced by pleas and groans.

Isaac liked being able to cover John's entire body with his. He liked throwing John around. He liked how John felt fragile, a thing to be cherished and protected—but what an illusion. John wasn't fragile at all.

Chapter Fourteen

JOHN CALLED IT "Loser Thanksgiving." In other words, it was John's Thanksgiving celebration for those unfortunates either without family nearby or, conversely, with family they didn't like. From Isaac's point of view, though, no one was losing anything at John's Thanksgiving party because not only was John cooking but he was also being cute. For instance, he currently stood in the kitchen by the open fridge, holding the last pumpkin beer of the season.

"Give that to me, Conlon." Adam, in a very Ramones-type getup of leather pants and black tee, extended his hand.

"I don't know, man." John wrinkled his nose. "I was thinking I might just pour it down the sink. One for my homies."

Football fans cheered from the living room where the Green Bay Packers played...someone. Isaac didn't care.

"John." Adam took a cautious step forward. "Put the beer down."

Tommy nudged Isaac as they watched the showdown, standing safely in the space between football and food with a nice view of the backyard, which was sadly getting deader by the moment. Without the leaves, Lothos had become a graveyard of grim trees—sharp fingers reaching out to grab hair, jackets, and sky.

"Maybe I'll just drink it myself." John flipped the lid with a bottle opener and took a sip. "Fuck, I am going to miss this."

"That's it." Adam lunged, and although John tried to juke out of his way, Adam's wingspan covered his entire escape route. John attempted a run in the other direction, but Adam latched onto the back of his sweater—an atrocious thing decorated with a rainbow turkey—and dragged a laughing John back into his arms. Maybe Adam was a little handsy while they tussled, but it was just Adam. Isaac had met the guy several times by then. Flirting with John was his part-time job, but he never tried to go further. They'd slept together once, and although sleeping with John only once would have killed Isaac, it seemed the two friends had just needed to get it out of their systems.

"Don't tell me you're getting jealous," Tommy said.

"No. It's just how they are."

Tommy drank IPA from a mug. Isaac could smell the piney hops from where he stood, over the scent of turkey in the oven. "I hear things are getting pretty serious in your forbidden tryst."

Isaac shook his head. "We're not from dueling families in Verona, Tommy."

"You're skyping with his parents tomorrow."

He watched John pour the pumpkin beer into two equal portions. Under the recessed kitchen lights, the little, round cups glowed like jack-o'-lanterns. "Well, I am going home with John for Christmas. I suppose they want to make sure I'm not a psychopath."

Tommy sighed. "But psychopaths look like everyone else."

He tilted his chin down and glared at Tommy from under his brows.

"I'll put in a good word for you. John's hot mom trusts my opinion." He tugged at the front of his Ohio State sweater as though adjusting a tie. "What about your family? Aren't they going to want to see you for the holidays?"

Isaac swished a bit of scotch around his mouth before swallowing. "They haven't spoken to me since I came out."

"What? Assholes."

"Not exactly."

Ten feet away, John and Adam chopped vegetables at the island. Meanwhile, Sasha the drag queen—dressed in full regalia for the occasion—stood behind and braided pieces of John's hair.

"My parents are conservative Southern Catholics," Isaac said. "Not only did their son come out as gay, but he also divorced his wife amidst massive scandal. It was too much to ask for them to stand by me."

"Bullshit. They're cowards."

"It wasn't—"

"Nope. I will not stand here and listen to you defend your asshole family." He clinked his beer against Isaac's glass. "You've got a new family now. A bunch of gays, drag queens, and bitter singles."

Isaac would not get choked up. He would *not*. "Thanks, Tommy."

"No problem."

"Speaking of family, shouldn't you be with yours in Columbus?"

Tommy shuddered and pulled his chin back until it almost disappeared into his neck. "Yeah, because I want to spend the day listening to my brother-in-law talk about computer engineering and how pot should be legal. I mean, it should be; I just don't want to debate over dinner. Then, my aunt will get too drunk and call my mom a whore. Yep, sounds fabulous. Plus, I don't know if you've noticed, but John makes the best food."

"I've noticed."

"Of course, you have." He poked Isaac in the side. "Dating John, how are you not fat? Oh, right, because you run two million miles every day." He wandered off toward the football game, so Isaac joined the kitchen crowd.

"John, do you need help?"

He looked up, half his head in braids. "You don't know how to cook."

"I could peel a potato?"

John snorted, and Adam pointed a paring knife. "Do not snot in the food!"

"You could snot all over me, baby." Sasha smirked and kept playing with John's hair. Her red sequined dress shimmered as a club mix played quietly from John's cell phone, his iTunes set to shuffle. She rolled her hips left to right—right against John's ass. "Come on, baby."

"No, I'm the chef, I—"

"Dance break!" Adam announced. He put down his knife and, instead of grabbing John, went right for Isaac. "Come on, big boy!"

Isaac just had time to put his drink down before being dragged into the living room. The reorganization was practically choreographed. Someone muted the football game. Someone else turned on the stereo. The coffee table was moved while Tommy, for his part, hid against a wall. As soon as a salsa beat started up, people hooted and hollered. John, despite being a foot shorter than Sasha, spun the drag queen and led her across the floor.

Adam put Isaac's hands in the right places. "I heard Cleo taught you how to do this, so just pretend I have tits."

True, Cleo had been the first to teach him, but John had perfected. They'd spent quite a few nights lately dancing around John's living room—but not surrounded by people. Isaac looked down at his feet for just a second to make sure he had the count and then did his best to lead a smiling Adam around the room. Even though Adam was a beanpole like John, Isaac wasn't used to leading someone his own height. At least he didn't step on any toes.

When the first song ended, everyone clapped, but another song started right away—a slow jitterbug. Adam reached for Isaac again, but John got in the way.

"Mind if I cut in?"

Adam rolled his eyes. "You would."

There was no way Isaac could hide their familiarity, not while dancing. He'd never cared for the activity before, hadn't seen much point. There were steps and songs and movements—but why? It just seemed like a lot to learn with no benefit.

Well, he understood dancing now. It was closeness and connection, foreplay with hips and hands. With John, dancing was a shared sway that almost always ended in bed.

"Damn, Isaac!" Adam hooted. "You've got moves."

Sasha snapped her fingers in the air, and John pressed the top of his head against Isaac's chest and laughed.

"OH, MY GOD. I'm never eating again." With the TV on mute, they all heard the sound of Tommy's stomach gurgling.

By then, it was just the three of them: Tommy, John, and Isaac. Which was why it was okay for John to be sitting between Isaac's legs on the floor while Isaac slowly untangled all the braids from his hair.

"I think he's hypnotized," Isaac said.

Tommy leaned forward and squinted. "John, quack like a duck."

"Quack."

"Give me a hundred bucks."

"Fuck off."

"Not hypnotized." Tommy leaned back and sipped from a tiny glass—one of a special set John reserved for "digestif." According to John, it was a French after-dinner tradition to drink a magic liqueur that aided digestion. That night's selection tasted of sweet pear. "Dinner was amazing, as usual. I can't believe you made turkey *and* duck."

"It was easy." He leaned his forehead against the side of Isaac's knee.

"Says Sleeping Beauty." The braids loosened, he put his fingers in John's hair and ruffled the locks free. "You look like you're going to an eighties prom."

John groaned and stood, stretching his arms over his head. No matter that he'd put away enough food to kill a cow, the trim bit of stomach revealed was flat as usual. "I'm going to bed. Tommy, you can stay as long as you want."

"I'll probably join everyone at the bars once I finish my tiny drink." He held up the tiny glass.

John leaned down and gave Tommy a hug. "Happy Thanksgiving."

"You too."

John shuffled toward the hall.

"Be there in a bit," Isaac said. When he realized he was checking out John's ass, he looked back toward the TV but felt Tommy watching him.

"You do make him really happy."

Isaac sighed, full on food and love. "Well, he makes me very happy too."

"You might want to decide what you're going to tell the school before your wedding."

Isaac smirked and closed his eyes. "Jesus. Yeah."

The light from the TV reflected off Tommy's glasses, hiding his eyes. "And I think people are starting to notice."

He sat up straight. "What? What people?"

"Well, Adam, for one," he said on a laugh. "And I quote, 'Wonder if Isaac eye fucks him that hard in bed.'"

He grumbled. "Anyone else?"

"No, Cleo's clueless. She should have that word on a T-shirt." Tommy studied the glass in his hand. "Just be a little more careful."

Isaac yawned, having caught the tired bug from John. "Pretty sure Janelle is onto us."

"Yeah, thanks to her wildly inappropriate relationship with John, she sees right through the guy. They're like two hipster-goth peas in a pod."

"She knew John and I had crushes on each other before we did."

"Crushes?" Tommy winced. "I know we work with kids, but you are way too old to have a crush on someone."

"But she was right: that's what it was. I did have a crush on John."

"You and everybody else." He finished his drink like it was some huge pour of scotch and not a sweet treat.

"Tommy. Thanks for looking out. Seriously."

"No worries." He stood. "I'm off. Good luck meeting the parents tomorrow. Word of warning, John and his mom go off on tangents in French, and it's..." He considered the ceiling. "Sexy as hell, honestly. Woman is a minx. I'm just waiting for his dad to die in some freak accident so I can move in."

"That's terrible."

"You haven't seen Mrs. Conlon."

Isaac walked him to the door. They shared a hug before Tommy walked off into the night, whistling. With the earlier help of guests, the kitchen shined. Isaac turned off the lights before washing up and slipping into bed. John immediately cooed and rolled over, nuzzling his face under Isaac's chin like a cat.

ISAAC AGREED TO meet with John, Anthony, and Janelle prior to their Tuesday night meeting to discuss cover art for *Being Frank*. They'd received quite a few submissions—good submissions—but it felt so heavy, choosing the look of their controversial magazine. The entire staff would be involved later that night, but for the time being, it was just the four of them.

Well, Anthony was late.

They stood around a big desk, staring at ink drawings and paintings and prints from graphic design students. It felt like every medium was represented, even photography, although those felt almost too real, especially one in particular—a mash-up of photos from *that day*, including a smiling photograph of Chris Frank.

John ran his hand over the back of his neck. "Fuck."

"Language," Isaac prompted.

"Shit. Sorry, Janelle."

She ran her fingertips over a splotch of dried red paint. Free-flowing black hair hid most of her face. "Just cuss in French. Then, nobody will know what you're saying."

John said something in French under his breath. He didn't sound like his mom. He spoke French with an American accent, according to her.

Sunday's Skype call had gone way easier than imagined. Sure, John had prefaced the whole thing by saying, "Don't be awkward," but Isaac concluded John had actually been talking to himself because his parents hadn't said much to Isaac. They hadn't pushed or prodded or mentioned any sort of age difference or questioned their jobs.

In fact, when the call had first come through, John's mother had said, "Oh, he's so handsome!" She was indeed beautiful, as Tommy had said, and spoke with an adorable accent Isaac had only heard in movies. There had been a mixture of French and English throughout. John's dad mostly smiled or rolled his eyes—must be hereditary—but their adoration for their only child had been palpable. They had waved and blown kisses. They'd asked Isaac for his Christmas list. When Mrs. Conlon—"Call me Maddy, please"—had started crying before hanging up, Isaac saw the resemblance. John did look just like her.

"This is going to be harder than I thought," John said.

Isaac nodded. "Who knew we'd get so many submissions?"

"And they just keep coming." John looked over his shoulder at the clock above the door. "Where's Anthony?"

Janelle picked up a photo of College Green and stared. She took a couple pieces of art with her and sat in a chair at the front of the room.

They heard the skid of Anthony's shoes before he came running in at a trot. "Dude, you aren't going to believe the shit I just heard."

John glanced back at Isaac, smiling, waiting for some comment about language, but Isaac would not give him the satisfaction.

"Well, it better be good considering you're twenty minutes late."

"I had to meet with my faculty advisor before this, and I was walking through the offices when I heard Meeks." Anthony tugged off his hat, and his huge hair expanded like a marshmallow in the microwave. "She was talking to someone about censoring books with violence. Like banning them from the program."

John's right eye twitched.

Isaac tapped his fist on the desk as if that would be enough distraction. "John."

John took a deep breath and audibly exhaled through his nose as his hands curled into fists. He closed his eyes and dug his teeth into his bottom lip.

"John," Isaac said. "Not your fight."

He whined and opened one eye to look at Isaac.

"But it is our fight, Dr. Twain," Anthony said. "Fight against oppression."

There was no way Isaac was stopping this. Book banning was up there as one of John's most hated things, along with the Carpenters, instant coffee, and light beer. It probably topped the list, tied with homophobia. Isaac knew John had gone to Washington, DC, years ago to protest censorship; he'd gone there again most recently with Janelle and Demi to speak out against hate crimes. Now, this. Censorship in his own school? Isaac almost felt sorry for Meeks.

"Just don't make it a screaming match," Isaac said.

"Duly noted. You and Janelle stay here and be brilliant. Anthony, into battle."

Anthony fist pumped and followed John out into the hall.

Skinny as he was, Isaac had no idea where John stored all his passion. Maybe he had an empty leg. It would certainly explain his alcohol tolerance.

Isaac grabbed a stack of art and sat at the desk next to Janelle. She wasn't flipping through the cover designs; she just stared at one—the photographic mash-up of the school, the shooting, and Chris Frank's face.

"You're fucking, you and John."

It felt like a slap to the face. "Jesus, Janelle."

"It's okay. You're both adults."

"When you talk to me like this, it makes me really uncomfortable. I am your teacher, an authority figure. I'm not your friend."

"I don't think John knows the difference, do you?"

Isaac had the urge to get the hell out of there, maybe join John in his battle against book banning, but Janelle kept talking.

"He was nice. Chris. Kind of weird, but quiet. He latched onto John because John didn't think of him differently, didn't think he was weird. I remember some kids were giving Chris shit one day in workshop. They were saying how boring his work was, and John said, 'If you're bored, you're boring.'" She tapped the photo. "He said it's up to our imaginations, when we write or read, to paint the image. Imagination is a powerful thing, for better or worse." She tugged on her earring until the skin of her ear drooped. "John is the only one who could have stood up that day—the only one Chris would have listened to. I imagine that's what bothers John the most."

"What?"

"He's a writer. And he didn't use the right words." She scraped a jagged nail against the photo and left a mark. "Demi and I were together for two years. Did you know that?"

"No."

"I first kissed her in the stairwell between the second and third floors of Ellis. She had a tongue ring, and I just wanted to see what it was like. I didn't mean to get attached."

A familiar sentiment.

"When was the first time you kissed John?"

Isaac shook his head. "I can't tell you that, Janelle." So they sat in silence, mulling over stacks of images that represented lost love, broken dreams, and death.

SOMETIMES, ISAAC THOUGHT it strange that his hips should fit so perfectly between John's thighs, considering their difference in size. During lovemaking, he occasionally stopped everything just to wrap his palms around John's slim waist and press his thumbs to the tender spot where hip met thigh. John always laughed when he did that and said, "I won't break, you big oaf." John would then paw at him until the kissing recommenced.

There was nothing playful about that night, no laughing interspersed between John's cracking voice. Outside the bedroom, his voice was rarely anything but strong and steady—even when overtaken by emotion. In the bedroom, that same voice went every which way, from high to low, breaking, shaking.

He wound his arms around Isaac's shoulders and his legs around his hips. He pulled him in for kiss after kiss until Isaac's mouth tasted more like John's than his own.

Their bodies flowed against each other, and Isaac gasped when John moved his hips in that certain way. John was not a good lover; he was an excellent lover. He observed, learned, and improved every time they touched. Isaac hadn't known about the sensitivity of his right earlobe until John. He'd never had someone climb on top of him and kiss his back, lick up his spine. He'd never had someone give and give. If he could, he imagined John would give away his skin and bones to make Isaac happy.

Hot breath against Isaac's face. "Where'd you go?"

"I'm here." He pressed his thumb to John's bottom lip until he opened and sucked.

Wet with saliva, Isaac ran his thumb down the center of John's neck. His Adam's apple bounced as he passed. Isaac stared at the pale skin there, with just a smattering of tiny freckles. He rested his palm across that tantalizing flesh.

"You can squeeze, you know, if you want." Based on the way John chewed his lips, he liked the idea—the idea of being choked. Just something new they might try.

But Isaac pulled away and shook his head. "No." He leaned back, dizzy all of a sudden.

The bed shifted as John sat up. "I know why you touch me there."

Isaac lilted to the side and moved his legs, no longer straddling John's hips. Sitting naked on the edge of the bed, he dragged his hands through his sweaty hair.

"Do you want to talk about it?" John asked.

"How could you ask me to choke you after…"

When Isaac didn't continue, John grabbed his hand roughly and twisted his wrist. Isaac gasped in protest—but John did not relent. He pressed Isaac's palm against his neck until Isaac's fingers grasped the vulnerable skin.

"Feel my pulse?"

It throbbed beneath Isaac's grip.

"He didn't pull the trigger."

"He could have," Isaac whispered.

"This part of my body is not sacred. It doesn't deserve worship."

"All of you deserves worship." Isaac tried to take his hand back, but John held tight.

"Sometimes you stare at this place like you're expecting to see blood. You have to stop." He dipped his chin and looked up from under his eyelashes. Isaac had seen that look before; John used it whenever he was trying to win an argument, probably because he knew it made him look like a wolf with a very good point.

"It's ridiculous," Isaac said, more to himself than to John. "I wasn't even here when it happened, but I think about it almost every day—think about what life would be like if I'd never met you."

John sighed and finally released Isaac's hand from around his throat. "Probably a lot fucking easier."

"But not half as interesting." He crawled back onto the bed and hovered.

John rested his hands on Isaac's chest. "Are we good?"

"Just because I have a morbid obsession with your neck doesn't mean I don't also find it incredibly attractive." He stuck the tip of his tongue right into the notch between John's collarbones.

John arched into the touch. "Maybe we should get the honey."

Isaac leaped from the bed in a rush for the kitchen. The only sounds were that of his bare feet on tile and John's quiet laughter.

Chapter Fifteen

HE ALMOST TRIPPED while trying to simultaneously put on his jacket and grab his satchel, but if he didn't hurry, Isaac was going to be late for his first Wednesday class. "John?" He hustled into the office to find John at his desk, forehead on the keyboard. "So writing is going well today?"

John groaned. Against the hard wood of the desk, the sound echoed like a banshee cry. "I used to like writing. I do not remember why."

Isaac picked up John's head by tugging on his hair. "Maybe you should take a break."

He moved his jaw left to right, stretching out the tension Isaac knew he held there. "I need to shower soon anyway."

"Did I get honey in your hair again?"

"Probably. I don't understand how you had the energy to shower at midnight. After round two, I passed the fuck out."

Isaac leaned on the edge of the desk. "I know. I had to roll you like a log to make space. Talk later?"

"Yeah, I'm going over to Janelle's on my way to campus. I really need her opinion on some of this cover art. It felt like she was barely paying attention at the meeting last night, and she's my go-to person, you know?"

Isaac winked. "I thought I was your go-to person."

John gagged. "Don't be gross in the morning."

He kissed John on the head. "I have to go. Love you."
John smiled.

Too much sex was the best form of insomnia Isaac had ever had, so despite the lack of sleep, he started his first class chipper and bordering on cheerful. The students probably thought he was high. He had found a groove—a rhythm. Miraculously, with the help of John and *Being Frank*, he was a teacher again.

Right in the middle of his roll, though, someone knocked at the door. Through the small cutout window, he caught a flash of Cleo's red hair and her big, blue eyes. "Excuse me, class." He opened the door and stuck his head out. "What's up?"

Before she covered her mouth, her lip trembled, and she started to cry.

ISAAC PULLED INTO the hospital parking lot and sprinted into the emergency room. He spotted Meeks immediately, talking in hushed tones on her cell phone. Her eyes widened when she saw Isaac but soon looked away, disinterested, as she continued having what looked like a heated debate. Isaac scanned the area in search of a familiar face, but all he saw was a curly-haired kid hugging herself and a construction worker with a bloody rag on his arm.

A nurse in green scrubs looked up from her desk. "Sir, can I—"

Tommy appeared from down a brightly lit hall, and Isaac ran to him, clinging to his shoulders. "Where is he?"

Tommy clung back. "I don't think he's okay, Isaac."

"Where...is...he?" Isaac growled out one word at a time.

"Back there." He glanced at a closed door. "I... He won't let anyone near him. He won't even... There's blood and..." He took forever to swallow. "He won't talk to me. I don't know..."

"Okay. I'll go."

"I don't want to lose him. I—"

"No." Isaac squeezed Tommy's shoulders. "We're not going to lose him. Go sit down, all right?" He moved beyond Tommy but paused. "Hey, did someone call her parents?"

Shoulders slumped, he said, "Yeah. Meeks. They're on their way, but they had to book a flight. It could be a while."

With a curt nod, Isaac went in search of John.

After doing a cursory scan of the emergency department hallways, Isaac found him sitting away from the main waiting area in a pool of shadow. Usually if John was in crisis, Isaac would run to him, but instead, Isaac froze on the tips of his feet as though hitting a concrete wall. For the second time since meeting John, he actually felt scared of him. It wasn't due to the blank expression or the way the shadows invaded the hollows of John's cheeks, no—it was the blood. His hands and chest were painted in it, his pastel pink shirt now a Rorschach test. *What do you see?* He could almost make out Janelle's face.

"John?"

He didn't move, so Isaac knelt slowly in front of him. Up close, there was a swash of blood across his cheekbone, too, and on his chin. They looked like fingerprints.

"John, can you hear me?" He wrapped his fingers around John's wrist and squeezed.

His eyes moved, at least. Although he looked at Isaac, there was no recognition.

"Hey, it's Isaac." He swallowed sorrow and forced a smile. "Remember me?"

John stared some more. Just as Isaac's vision started going fuzzy with tears, he nodded. "How did you know to come here?"

"Cleo." He plucked a curl from the center of John's forehead and pushed it back over his brow. "Would you come to the bathroom with me, John?"

His thin fingers trembled when he looked down at them, but he nodded again.

With one arm around his shoulders, Isaac led John the twenty steps to the men's restroom. ER staff tried not to stare as they went. Inside, beneath the too-bright overhead light, Janelle's blood looked like something out of a B-horror film. He leaned John against the wall, away from the mirror, and pulled a stack of paper towels from the dispenser. He went for John's face first, wetting the cloths and gently pressing them against his skin. He focused on the task, busied himself with the mundane, because otherwise, Isaac feared he would start screaming. John merely blinked at his attentions.

Once his face was clean, Isaac took both John's hands in his and held them under the faucet. Water ran red, then pink, as he added more soap to the mix—and more soap. Isaac never knew blood was so hard to wash off. Inside, blood kept us alive; outside, it stained skin, clothes, and minds.

As Isaac massaged suds into John's nails, John's hands suddenly squeezed. Isaac looked up, expecting finally some show of emotion, but no, John was still haunted and empty.

"I didn't spend the summer with my family in Wisconsin," he said. "I spent it in a psych ward."

Isaac dropped his head, nodding. He released one of John's hands, and despite the soap and blood, covered his eyes as the tears came. He dragged John into his arms and cried against his hair, even though John barely hugged him back. John was a statue.

They stepped away when the door opened—and just in time since Meeks walked in. "The nurses said I'd find you in here. John, we need to talk."

John took a shuffling step forward, but Isaac halted him with a hand on his upper arm. "Tomorrow," he said.

She scoffed. "What are you, Twain, his keeper?"

"No, I'm his friend."

She put both hands in the air and then brushed them across her hips. "Fine. Whatever." Her over-made-up face didn't move, frozen in a strained expression of discontent. "John, my office at eight a.m. And pull yourself together." Her high heels clicked as she stomped away.

MEEKS CANCELED ALL English Department classes for the remainder of the week. Isaac imagined she wanted people to think she was being sympathetic, but in reality, he guessed she was trying to stop the spread of gossip on a campus just waiting for more bad news.

At John's house, Isaac left Tommy in the kitchen and ushered John into the bathroom, where he stripped off his bloodstained clothes. He turned on the water, warm, and took off his own clothes, too, before guiding John under the spray. Isaac reached for John's fancy shampoo and rubbed his head until his curls turned white.

By the time he'd finished, John's skin was finally clean. He wrapped his arms around himself while Isaac toweled him off. Once, John leaned up on his toes and kissed Isaac's cheek. They shared a few breaths. Despite the lack of words, it was the loudest conversation they'd had in weeks.

In the bedroom, Isaac dressed John in his own pajamas and wasn't sure why. Isaac's sweatshirt hung low around John's throat and swallowed his hands. The plaid bottoms pooled over his feet on the floor, hiding even his toes. Isaac took the afghan from the bottom of the bed and wrapped it around John's shoulders. If only he could keep John warm, maybe he could keep John safe.

"Do you want to sleep?" Isaac asked.

John shook his head and roamed, in all his excess fabric, to the living room, where he slumped onto the couch—and slumped some more until only the top half of his face and his shower-damp curls remained visible.

Tommy waited in the kitchen, fists wrapped around the edges of the island as though he wanted to tear the whole thing apart.

Isaac opened cupboards. He found chamomile tea first and then, whiskey. He and Tommy shared a look before Isaac put the tea away and reached for three rocks glasses. He poured two shots. Without saying a word, both men threw theirs back. Isaac poured another round and a third for John and moved to the living room.

John's pale hand sprang from the nest of fabric and grabbed the whiskey, but he didn't drink it—just sat there with it in his hand. Isaac put his arm around him, while Tommy sat in the recliner by the back door.

Eventually, John swallowed the whiskey. Eventually, he leaned his head on Isaac's shoulder, which was when silence was finally broken.

"We're here," Isaac said before the silence returned.

ISAAC CLOSED THE bedroom door quietly. It was only six thirty, but the winter sun had already sunk and John had said he was tired. It was the only thing he'd said all afternoon.

Tommy poked at a cold, half-eaten piece of pizza on the counter. They'd ordered delivery in the middle of the afternoon once the grumbles of their stomachs had interrupted the horrible stillness in the cozy house that was rarely still.

Like opponents at a chessboard, Isaac and Tommy stood across from each other.

"What happened?" Isaac asked.

"Janelle slit her wrists, and John found her."

Saying it out loud made Isaac's assumptions die. He buried them with the urge to run to John's bedroom and never let go. "And she's still alive."

"Yes."

"Was there a note?"

"I don't think so." Tommy slid the pizza away. "By the time I got to the hospital, John was catatonic. I mean, you saw him."

Yes, and the image of John motionless, covered in blood, would haunt Isaac for months. "Do you know where he really was this summer?"

Tommy deflated. Spine curled, he rested his elbows on the counter and dug his fingers into his hair. "Yes."

"Why didn't you tell me?"

"It was never my business to tell."

"Do you know why he was hospitalized?" Isaac asked.

Tommy put one hand on his hip and whacked the island. "Goddamn it, Isaac. How would he not be hospitalized? Fuck!" He paced away and paced back just as fast. "You don't know what it was like for him. A bunch of kids get shot, and everyone's calling him a hero? What he did was fucking insane, and yes, it probably saved lives, but he had to watch Chris shoot himself in the head. And the media? Christ!" He looked up as though calling for said deity. "They were all over this town, all over John. God, they followed him everywhere. They wanted to know everything about him. 'What did you say to the shooter? What were his last words?' Thing that pissed John off the most was that they stopped using Chris's name; he was just 'the shooter.' And John never told those vultures a thing. To this day, no one knows anything about those final seconds—not even me."

He stepped closer, almost invading Isaac's space with anger that radiated like flames. "Even worse, once this goddamn country got a look at John Conlon, they swooned. Forget about the dead kids; look how handsome the hero is. He was getting love letters from all over the country. Marriage proposals, as if his biggest accomplishment was being a heartthrob when people were dead." Tommy paced away again, this time facing their reflections in the back glass door. "After a while, he couldn't even go outside anymore. I used to have to bring him food, and he would just... The way he is today, he was like that for weeks before he made the decision to go away. He had to find some hospital in Nowhere, South Dakota, so they wouldn't find him. We are the only ones who know—us, his parents, and his shrink. Not the school. Not the media, thank Christ. I have been watching him like a hawk since the beginning of the semester, and I get glimmers...God." He growled and covered his face. "I get glimpses of who he used to be." His chest lurched on a sob, but before Isaac could react, John's voice interrupted.

"Hey. Assholes." He stood in the doorway, holding his phone. "What part of 'I'm tired' did you not understand, Shouty McShouterson?"

Tommy's sob turned into a bark of laughter. "God, how much of that did you hear?"

"Enough." John shuffled forward and rubbed Tommy's back while watching Isaac. "Any questions?"

"Would you ever hurt yourself?" Isaac asked.

John hesitated and rubbed his lips together. "I don't think so."

At that admission, Tommy grabbed onto John's arm and dragged him into a hug. "You better not."

John's cell phone vibrated on the island, so Isaac took a glance. "It's Anthony."

"Yeah, he's been texting. Janelle's stable, but she's still not awake."

"You saved her life," Tommy mumbled against John's shoulder.

"Let's not put anymore lives on my head, okay?" John pulled away and smiled at Tommy. "Look at you. You haven't cried like this since Michigan beat Ohio State in the Rose Bowl."

"God, don't remind me."

"Are you okay to go home?" John asked.

Tommy took off his glasses and wiped his eyes. "Can I stay on your couch?"

"Of course." John reached for Isaac's hand and squeezed. "I don't think I'm going to be able to sleep tonight, so why don't we drag blankets in from the bedroom and have a slumber party? Watch a movie or something?"

Isaac hadn't realized how much he'd missed the sound of John's voice all day until right then.

Ten minutes later, they'd built a blanket and pillow fort on the living room floor. On the TV screen, Tom Hanks played nosey neighbor in *The 'Burbs*. John and Tommy knew all the punch lines, but even as they recited, they still laughed. Distracted, Isaac dug around beneath the blankets and past the overlarge hoodie until he could pull John close by his bare skin. He turned down a glass when Tommy poured whiskey and eventually fell asleep wrapped around a still awake John quoting Bruce Dern.

FOR THE DURATION of John's early morning meeting with Meeks, Isaac hid in his office and walked in circles simply because it would be obvious if he stood with his nose pressed against her door. He only had to pace for twenty minutes before a quiet knock preceded John, who looked like a hungover beatnik poet. He wore the newsboy cap Isaac knew he only used on "bad hair days," black skinny jeans, and his gray blazer over a V-neck tee. Maybe he looked more French than beatnik.

"What'd she say?"

"Wanted to know if I saw any warning signs." He shrugged. "And I have no idea."

"What kind of warning signs?"

He drooped into Isaac's guest chair. "The usual bullshit. Negative talk, substance abuse, loss of interest. I mean, I guess I saw those things, but that's just Janelle. She's emo as fuck, but I never thought she'd try this again."

"Her black bracelets."

John steepled his fingers over his nose and spoke from between his palms. "She slit her wrist when she was thirteen when she realized she was gay. Just the one wrist, not like—Jesus, it was like she was trying to saw her arms off yesterday, Isaac." His cell phone vibrated in his back pocket, and he leaned forward to grab it. "At protests, she's spoken out to other gay kids about how suicide is not the answer. I don't get why she did this." He tapped at his phone. "Anthony's at the hospital." He muttered a "fuck" from behind closed eyes. "He says Janelle's parents are there and being awful."

When John stood, Isaac latched onto his arm. "It's not your responsibility."

He tugged his arm away. "Yes. It is."

Isaac reached for his suit coat on the back of his chair. "Then, I'm coming with you."

John snickered and squeezed the bridge of his nose. "It's *really* not *your* responsibility."

"Don't talk to me like I'm not part of this."

John's volume jumped. "You're not! You're six months late to the party, man."

Isaac's mouth dropped open on a "Wow." He leaned back against his desk and crossed his arms. "Do you resent me for that?"

John's forehead wrinkled when he looked outside, out at the naked sycamore and the beginnings of College Green. He whispered, "Sometimes." His throat heaved on an audible swallow. "Sometimes I wish you'd been here. But then, I hate myself because what if you had been here, and what if you were dead? Janelle lost Demi; what if I'd lost you?"

Isaac had considered it before, the notion of never having met John—of John's summer funeral, of his slim body in a box. The weight of this death that never happened still suffocated Isaac on occasion—but the ever-strengthening flicker of optimism knew better. "I was supposed to meet you," he said. "There was never any question. I was waiting to find you."

John shook his head. "No, I don't deserve that."

"Well, I do," Isaac said as the ghosts of Elizabeth and Simon released his heart and disappeared to the dark hovel where regrets go to die.

NO MATTER HOW clean they claimed to be, hospitals smelled like sick people—and stale food—but mostly sick people. Despite the stench, Isaac breathed resolutely through his nose so as not to swallow the air around him and taste illness, despair. They met Anthony in the waiting room, half his huge hair flattened from probably sleeping in a hospital chair.

"She won't wake up, but they won't even let me see her, man." He started walking, and they followed rapidly behind.

John eyed his clothes. "Well, your T-shirt is pretty much a conservative nightmare." All it said was "I'm rooting for everyone black."

Anthony buttoned his red cardigan as they turned down a couple stinking hallways. Someone wept from behind a green curtain. After scurrying past a nurse's desk, Anthony stopped and pointed to a handsome middle-aged couple whispering back and forth. Still ruffled from the panicked flight, their expensive clothes didn't sit quite right on their bodies. The woman had Janelle's eyes, but that was where the resemblance stopped. Both blond, Janelle apparently dyed her long, black hair, and she would never wear pastel.

"Mr. and Mrs. Houcks?"

They turned at the sound of John's voice.

"I'm John Conlon, one of Janelle's teachers."

Janelle's father grew five inches. "Oh, we know who you are, Mr. Conlon. Dr. Meeks told us everything. A literary magazine about the shooting? Are you insane or just stupid?"

"Look, it was—"

"No, you listen to me." Janelle's father pointed a fat finger. "This is on you. My little girl lost her best friend, and you would shove it in her face. These children need to be protected from monsters like you. We let her come across the country for school because our little girl wanted to learn from you, her favorite author, and what happened? She got all these crazy ideas about girls kissing girls. She writes terrifying stories about murderers and deviants. Then, she almost gets shot, and now, this!"

The entire hallway turned to look.

"My little girl might go to hell because of you."

Vision blurry with rage, Isaac opened his mouth to argue, but John beat him to it.

"Excuse me if I disagree."

Mr. Houcks clapped his hands once. "Oh, so he has a voice."

"Yes, he has a voice," Isaac said, but John put a hand on his chest to keep him back.

He took a step forward, and Houcks took a step away like John carried a disease he didn't want. "You don't even know your daughter. She didn't come to Hambden just to learn from me; she came here to get away from you. You still treat her like some bubblegum princess who's going to marry a Ken doll!"

Mrs. Houcks tugged on her husband's arm when he tried to lurch forward, but Isaac lurched forward, too, holding his hands out between the man he loved and the angry father who wanted to rip him apart.

"And news flash, stop calling Demi her best friend. Demi was Janelle's girlfriend, and they were in love."

Janelle's mom shouted, "My little girl is not some filthy lesbian."

"She spends enough time with me," John said. "I hear the gay is catching!"

"Why, you little son of a—"

Isaac had to shove against Mr. Houcks to keep a full brawl from breaking out in intensive care.

Anthony didn't help when he pointed at John and yelled, "Fight him, man! Fuck, yeah!"

"Stay away from my daughter!" Houcks kept pushing against Isaac until a confused security guard showed up and told everyone to calm down. "Arrest him," Houcks cried. "He should be arrested." But there was no truth to it, no legal reason. As Houcks leaned back against his wife, face crumpled in grief, Isaac took hold of John's lapel and pulled him away from the confused, broken couple who'd almost lost their daughter twice.

Halfway down the hall, they heard Janelle's dad saying, "Monsters."

Bitter wind tugged at their coats outside, and the sun didn't dare show its face.

John froze on the pavement and threw his hat on the ground. "Oh, my God, what did I just do?"

Isaac put his hand on his own chest; his heart thumped like a heavy metal drum. "Probably got us both fired. *The gay is catching?* What the fuck were you thinking?"

"He was thinking Janelle deserves better than those two bigots for parents."

"Anthony!"

The kid's eyes went wide at the volume of Isaac's voice.

"I'm sorry," Isaac said. "Just... Go back inside. Please."

"Damn," he said but did as told.

"John, have you lost your mind?" Isaac asked.

John sat on the ice-cold sidewalk and pulled his knees into his chest. He hid behind his hair. "I don't want to do this anymore."

Isaac went down on one knee next to him. "What are you talking about?"

"I don't want to fight anymore, Isaac." He smashed his face against Isaac's chest and sobbed. "I'm so tired."

"Okay." He put one hand on the back of John's neck and used the other to rub his quaking shoulders as quiet weeping turned to silent vibrations of pain. "Let's get you home."

ISAAC'S LUNGS BURNED with every breath as he sprinted through the streets of Lothos. A few snowflakes dawdled at eye level before hitting the ground, the frozen ghosts of rain.

He'd left John with Tommy back at the house because he needed a moment too—a moment to admit he was scared. Janelle's father was surely making a fuss, probably talking to Meeks, but Isaac didn't worry about his job anymore. Who cared about his stupid job if John was falling apart in front of him?

John's summer in the psych ward allowed him to go outside again and return to Hambden as beloved teacher and friend. Then, Isaac came along, with all his closeted hang-ups and memories of exes and abortions. Isaac just had to kiss him in a Columbus hotel room. Isaac had to put him through hell with Simon, with Tommy, perhaps even within John's own mind, bowed beneath the weight of their secret—a secret that had started with sex and accidentally grown into love, for Isaac, at least. Maybe John didn't love him. Maybe John would be better off without him.

But, oh, the selfishness of man. Isaac couldn't imagine his life without John.

Barely paying attention to his route, he stopped when he recognized the cemetery. He'd been there once before, to the place with the weeping angel. Frozen pieces of grass crunched beneath his running shoes as he wiped the sweat from his brow. Unlike in October, the air had no smell. It just smelled cold.

Isaac stared up at the old marble angel with her somber expression, her face once clean white but now dark gray and covered in lacelike turquoise moss. He traced his finger down one of her cheeks, stained with tears, and realized she reminded him of John—standing there strong and tall despite the cold that threatened, beautiful in her melancholy. Then, he knelt.

"Hail Mary, full of grace, the Lord is with thee. Blessed art thou among women, and blessed is the fruit of thy womb, Jesus. Holy Mary, Mother of God, pray for us sinners, now and at the hour of our death." He crossed himself. "Hail Mary, full of grace, the Lord is with thee..."

The tombstones listened as the angel wept.

AS SOON AS he walked in, soaked with sweat and yet chilled to the bone, he heard John's voice from the living room. Isaac went to the kitchen for a glass of water but halted when he realized both Tommy and Cleo stood at the island, staring at him.

"Dr. Twain?" Cleo asked. She brushed loose pieces of hair out of her face.

"Uh."

"They're fucking," Tommy said.

Isaac rolled his eyes. "We're not just fucking, Tommy. I love him."

"Oh, God," Cleo whispered. "The Brown-Lancaster Debacle." She looked around the room as though searching for sense. None was apparently forthcoming, because she remained standing there, confused, in a long sweater dress and winter coat.

John walked in and threw his phone on the counter. The sound made them all jump.

"Do you still have a job?" Tommy asked.

"Barely. Meeks said this isn't the time for further upheaval. Fuck, let's get drunk."

"Hang on." Isaac stepped forward. "John, can I talk to you for a second?"

He nodded shakily before pulling a glass down from above the sink, filling it with water, and handing it to Isaac. Isaac took a sip and set the glass on the counter, tugging John gently by his shirt into the hallway. He whispered, "I think you should go see your therapist."

John laughed under his breath. "Right now?"

There it was: the façade of levity that made Isaac's blood run cold.

"I think this would be a really good time, yes," Isaac said.

John looked away and ran his hand over the back of his head. "I think I really need a drink."

"John, please—"

He turned and walked away. "Shower and meet us at Joe's, okay? *Allons-y!*" he announced to his cohorts in the kitchen.

Cleo scurried after him, but Tommy paused in the hallway long enough to say, "I'll keep an eye on him. Just hurry up."

The shower was wasted because even though Isaac washed away the sweat from his run, he sprinted down John's hill and onto Union Street. By the time he walked into Joe's, the snow fell with ambition, and Tommy and John discussed something at the bar. Two o'clock drinking during a snowstorm was apparently reserved for the desperate and disturbed, as the bar was empty except for their group.

Before Isaac could join the boys' conversation, John handed him a bourbon-filled rocks glass and waved him to a back table where Cleo sat poking at a piece of pink chalk. He slid in across from her but kept his eyes on John.

"Look at me," she said over the sound of the jukebox, Rolling Stones.

He did as bid.

She moved her gin and tonic back and forth. "Are you actually gay, or is this one of those clichéd I'm-gay-for-one-person things?"

He tried not to chug his Knob Creek. "I'm definitely gay."

She poked at the table. "I did not see this coming."

He watched John have an animated conversation he couldn't hear.

"Do you really love him?" she asked. "Like you said?"

"I love him so much that I feel like I'm going crazy."

This admittance only seemed to upset her. "Well, is one of you going to quit your job? Because you can't. You're both really good teachers, and the school needs you, and I will not let you both get fired and destroyed, and—"

"Honestly, Cleo, my job is the least of my worries today."

She side-eyed John. "He'll be okay. He's always okay."

"I really don't think that's true." He noticed the unfamiliar slump of her shoulders and the lack of makeup. "Are *you* okay?"

"No," she said as if it were the most obvious thing in the world. She stirred her drink and poked at the lime but didn't consume. "I know there's supposedly a reason for everything and all the bad stuff just makes us stronger, but... What the hell, Dr. Twain? How come such shitty things are happening to good people?"

"I can't answer that." He paused. "But I did pray for the first time in five years today."

"Why?"

He looked toward John just in time to watch him down a shot of something dark. "I don't know. Maybe I'm tired of pretending I have control over anything. People make decisions, and everyone else has to live with the consequences. Maybe I was praying for people to start making the right decisions."

John and Tommy slid in on either side of their booth and handed out shots. Nobody asked about the contents, but everyone drank.

WITH A TONGUE like sandpaper and mouth syrup sweet, Isaac woke in the middle of the night to an empty bed. His head already pounded with the impending hangover, thanks to overindulgence at Joe's and then back at John's. He wasn't sure what time it had been when Tommy and Cleo had gone home, but Isaac had passed out soon after. He hadn't "passed out" in years. He remembered John climbing into bed at some point. They hadn't touched, but he'd felt John's slight weight dip the bed and the added warmth of his body. Now, John was gone.

Isaac burped vomit when he sat up and had to swallow several times to be certain he wasn't about to hurl all over John's floor. He stumbled from the bedroom and down the hall in the direction of the only light in the house.

John sat at the kitchen table, facing away. The computer glow lit the edges of his hair, but other than that, he was merely a black silhouette.

Isaac almost said his name but stopped when he recognized the video on John's computer screen. He'd seen it months ago when he'd first done research into the Hambden shooting and the "Hambden hero." It was the video of Chris Frank holding a gun on John but then shooting himself.

It played to the end, and John repeated it.

It played to the end. John repeated it.

Despite his still-drunk stupor, Isaac had the urge to run to John and slam the computer shut. Instead, he clung silently to the wall as Chris Frank died over and over again.

Chapter Sixteen

ANTHONY, WHO HAD apparently snuck into Janelle's hospital room in the middle of the night, texted first thing to tell John she wanted to see him. Although John had suggested he go alone, Isaac had refused. True, he'd let John watch that video on repeat for an hour. Eventually, John had closed the damn laptop, turned around, and said, "I didn't know you were there," before nonchalantly kissing Isaac's cheek, walking by, and climbing back into bed. But Isaac didn't want John anywhere near Mr. and Mrs. Houcks without his protection.

Sitting in the hallway, Janelle's parents didn't say anything when they walked by. They just stared, and John resolutely looked straight ahead. Anthony had gone, he said, "to get her some real food," so Janelle sat alone when they arrived. If not for the big, white bandages, she would have looked no different than usual—same smudged, black eye makeup, chipped nails, and straight, black hair.

John pulled one hand from his pocket and poked the back of her hand, a childish gesture that made him look like a kid asking for his first kiss. "Hey."

"I didn't want you to save me," she said.

"I don't care."

They spoke just below library volume.

"I'll do it again," she said.

John's sudden weave was slight, but he would have hit the floor if Isaac hadn't been there to catch him with a strong hand on his elbow. John glanced up at him once before swallowing and clearing his throat. "Why?"

Her top lip curled. "Because I hate this world. And I miss her."

"Demi wouldn't want you to—"

Her head tilted up like a marionette on a string. "Isaac, if John were gone, what would you do?"

John took a step forward, close to her bed. "Janelle—"

She snarled, "I want him to tell me what he would do if you were dead. You love him, Isaac. What would you do? Tell me."

He took a step around to John's side so he could look down at the face of the man he knew so well: the bedroom eyes, rose-petal pout, and chin that never needed shaving, but also the dark circles of exhaustion and hollow cheeks. When was the last time John had eaten? Careless of consequence, Isaac touched John's jaw. "I was dead before I met you, but even if you leave me, that's not happening again," he said.

Janelle snickered. "Easy for you to say now when you can still hold him. When you don't know what he sounds like calling for help. When you don't know what his blood feels like." Her hands shook as she curled them against her chest.

"We should get her nurse," Isaac said.

"Why did you come back, John?" She sang her words like a playground taunt. "How could you come back here after what happened? *You* of all people?"

"It's my home."

She stared at the opposite wall, unseeing. "Well, your home is shit. It's nothing but a dark corridor with no way out. You feel it. I know you do. The hell of this place."

John had never looked more like a man made of concrete. "Janelle, I know what you're going through, but—"

"No." Her eyes were vacant as a baby doll's. "I'm going home with my parents back to Oregon. I'm quitting school," she said. "I can't be here anymore. I can't read their stupid stories. I don't want to see Demi everywhere I look, so I will never think about this place or you again. I'm sorry I ever read your books. I'm sorry they brought me here. I'm sorry I ever met you, John. So go." Her head tilted like she might fall asleep, and in some parody of a ghost story, the room felt colder.

John opened his mouth to speak, but Isaac tugged on his coat. He tugged some more until John began to follow, and Isaac led him to the door. Janelle's singsong voice found them again as they crossed the threshold.

"What did you say to Chris on the Green, John? What did you say?"

John's small hand curled in the front of Isaac's shirt as he stared back at the sick girl. He gagged once before Isaac wrapped his arm around the front of John's chest and dragged him away from the scent of illness and death.

JOHN DIDN'T SPEAK until they got back to his house. He barely moved on the car ride home, just studied his upturned palms as though reading a fortune. Once inside, he shuffled down the foyer and into the kitchen, planting his fists against the island, muttering, "It's her parents. Pouring poison in her ear. That's wasn't— Janelle isn't— No, I know her. She's not—"

"What did you say to him on College Green?"

John's head snapped up, eyes wide. "What the hell did you just say to me?"

Isaac was done with secrets. All his life, secrets had protected him, kept him safe, until they destroyed his marriage, his career, and his life. "Tell me."

He shook his head. "I've never told anyone. Why the fuck would I tell you?"

"Because it's me." He put his hand on his own chest but remained across the kitchen, for fear of spooking John with proximity when his words threatened enough. "It's me, John."

"And who are you, huh?" John crossed his arms in a semblance of armor. "You show up here in my house." He pointed to the library. "You become my friend, then my lover, and now, what? Are you my therapist?"

"I'm the man who loves you."

John tilted his head back and closed his eyes. "Then, why would you ask me that question?"

"Because I want to know everything about you, even the worst."

"No, you don't." John sucked in a sob and covered his mouth with his hand. When Isaac took a step forward, John took a step back. "Don't come near me. I don't deserve all that you've given me, please, Isaac. You should leave."

"No. Talk to me." Even if Isaac wasn't ready, even if he already suspected he knew what had happened between John and Chris on College Green, Isaac needed John to say it—for both of them.

John shoved his hands in his pockets. "Do you know you shower after every time we fuck? Almost like you can feel something awful in my skin?"

Isaac opened his mouth to debate but stopped. He'd showered after he and Patrick had made love in college. He'd showered after every one-night stand, the hotter the water the better. He'd showered after Simon, and now, he showered after John. "That was never about you," he said.

"No." John scratched his eyebrow. "Your stupid Catholic shit, I know that. I don't mind it really. I almost like it—the thought that my ugliness isn't washing off on you."

"John—"

"I've spent my life writing books to help troubled kids, and"—his lips trembled—"I couldn't help the one standing right in front of me. Now, I hate the books. I can barely stand to look at them. They shout at me from the bookcase, from the page. They remind me how I failed."

Despite the tense bubble surrounding John, Isaac forced his feet to break through, close enough to put his hands on John's unsteady shoulders. "You saved lives. God knows how many. You did what you had to."

"I told Chris to kill himself, Isaac."

He pressed his lips against John's and sucked the words into his own mouth as though consuming them would swallow the guilt.

"I told him to kill himself because it was only going to get worse. I didn't care if I died that day; that's not why I did it. I just wanted him to know the truth." His chest shook as the tears came, tears that started so small and tremulous, then matured into loud howls that stole John's physical strength. He fell to the floor on his knees, and Isaac joined him, arms around shoulders that shook and hands that grasped. "I wish sometimes he'd just shot me."

"God." Isaac dug his fingers into John's hair and held him so close it probably hurt. "Don't say that."

"I'm not a hero. I'm a fucking monster."

Isaac closed his eyes and shook his head. He wanted to run from the house, drag John with him, and rewind back to before June. Start over, him and John, without the added weight of that day—that stupid day in the sun. John had said what he'd thought needed saying to Chris Frank, and now that he'd admitted it to Isaac, Isaac knew he'd been just waiting to end up here with truths like blood puddles on the floor.

I told Chris to kill himself.

Had Isaac seen those words in John's eyes before? Had he felt those words pressed into his naked skin? Yes. Yes, again and again, but now, the words were free. Maybe John could be free too.

He wiped his soaking face on Isaac's shirt. "I think I should be punished, but I don't know how."

"You've punished yourself enough."

"You shouldn't love me. God, why do you love me?"

Isaac could have given a million reasons. He could have talked about John's looks, the way his body felt in bed. Or the way John laughed with his mouth open wide. The way he wrote, the way he cooked, or the way he wore Converse shoes even in the snow. The way he gave all of himself to try to save other people, even if he didn't succeed.

Instead, Isaac whispered, "Because you're my hero."

John laughed and then wept against the side of his face. They stayed wrapped together on the kitchen floor until John sniffled to sleep. Isaac carried him to the bedroom and tucked him in tight before sitting in John's living room. In the midafternoon, with the snow outside, the light glowed white, painting every surface in the crisp clean of winter. The house was Isaac's home—John was his home—and he would fight for both.

Chapter Seventeen

ON THE PHONE, John's mother sounded steady and calm. She called Isaac "mon cheri," which made John complain, "But that's my nickname." She promised to make the necessary arrangements and didn't ask too many questions. More than anything, she wanted to make sure her son was safe, and that, Isaac could guarantee. John hadn't left Isaac's sight once over the past twelve hours.

John sat on the edge of his bed next to his suitcase as Isaac pulled things from drawers. Isaac knew which shirts were John's favorites. He knew where to find underwear and socks. In the bathroom, he knew to grab John's toothbrush and mouth guard—his "dentures," as they jokingly called it. He even packed John's shampoo and lotion, although Isaac put a bit of the witch hazel balm in a smaller container that he could keep for when the coming nights without John might howl like ghosts.

Satisfied with his work, Isaac zipped the suitcase closed. John grabbed his hand and pulled until Isaac got the message and sat next to him. John leaned his full body weight against Isaac and hid his face against Isaac's chest.

"Hey, it's not forever." Isaac kept telling himself that, so he thought John should hear it, too, no matter that it did little to dwindle the ache in his chest, the echo like hunger in his tummy.

John mumbled something.

Isaac felt warm breath against his skin so leaned closer. "What?"

"I don't want to leave you," he said.

"Don't think of it that way." Isaac pulled back so he could tilt John's chin up and stare. "You're not leaving me. You're leaving Lothos to get help, but I will be here when you get back."

"What if you forget about me?"

He kissed John's forehead. "How could I forget about you when I'm keeping an eye on your house and walking your streets? Everything here reminds me of you. Not to mention the fact that you're taking half my heart with you to South Dakota; you know that, right?"

"God, you're so maudlin."

Isaac gave him a playful shake.

"I'm sorry for..." John's eyebrows squeezed together.

Isaac knew he was going to say Chris's name, but it was over. It was past, so he cut him off. "We're good. Everything is good."

John's jaw clenched. "Watch out for Tommy and Cleo?"

"Yeah." He touched John's hair—couldn't stop really.

"Are you seriously petting me?" John asked.

"I know I'm supposed to be the strong, supportive boyfriend right now, but I am going to miss the hell out of you."

John pitched forward, and Isaac caught the familiar weight. His John: skin and bones that never felt sharp but always soft and welcoming. Slim hips Isaac could hold in the palms of his hands. Wild hair and even wilder eyes and a mouth that could cause both pleasure and pain.

"I fucking love you," John whispered.

Isaac held John even tighter.

"I've loved you for so long. I don't know why I didn't say it."

"It doesn't matter," Isaac said as salt stung his eyes. "I love you too."

THE ENTIRE STAFF of *Being Frank* stared at Isaac as if he had all the answers, but he didn't—not even close. Isaac was more lost than ever, having put John on a plane the day prior for his extended leave of absence. He was going back to the "nut house," as John so lightly put it. Isaac had stayed at John's house the night before and barely slept. The whole house felt wrong with him gone. Isaac had never realized how quiet it was on top of that damn hill.

"Well." He congratulated himself on such a strong opening.

"How's Janelle?" a mousy girl asked from the back.

"As far as I know, she went back to Oregon with her parents on Saturday."

Anthony, hiding under a hood, nodded to confirm. Isaac hadn't slept the night before, but Anthony looked like he hadn't slept in days. Maybe he hadn't. His best friend was gone—alive but possibly never the same—and here he was, trying to talk about school.

"And what about John?" Anthony lifted his head just enough to be heard.

Isaac crossed his arms, visibly protecting his heart. "He's on temporary leave, getting some help. I don't know how long he'll be gone."

Collectively, shoulders dropped. From where he stood, Isaac could just make out the snow-covered altar on College Green. He took a deep breath, held it, and let it out. "After all that's happened, I assume people are going to expect us to shut this down. They might say it would be in poor taste to continue. But I disagree."

Anthony flipped his hood back. "You do?"

"It's callous of me to say I understand what happened to all of you last June. I don't. But if there's one thing I've learned at my ancient age—" He tried to smile. "—if I've learned anything, it's that running away from the horrible things that happen to us is a race that never ends. You could run your whole life from the memory of this, but eventually, you're going to get tired of running, and that's when you'll fall apart. If we face this now, together— remember all of it—maybe we can start to heal. And not just us; maybe we can heal the whole school."

"That is some idealistic bullshit, Dr. Twain." Anthony smirked and chewed on the string from his hoodie. "But I can dig it."

"Gee. Thanks, Anthony."

"With John gone, are you going to fight our battles now?"

"Tooth and nail."

Anthony ducked again beneath his hood. "I want to add John and Janelle to the dedication page since we lost them too."

Isaac shook his head. "They're not lost. They're just...rerouting." He blinked at his own word choice. He'd been rerouting for years but had finally reached his destination.

Chapter Eighteen

THE FIRST WEEK without John was torture. They talked on the phone once, but John mostly just yawned. He was having trouble sleeping, he said.

The first month without him felt like being slowly crushed by a huge rock. Isaac kept up appearances because he had to. He'd inadvertently become the student's John replacement—a bigger, blonder, surlier clone of the young teacher they all adored. When Meeks blithely mentioned the word "censorship" at a faculty meeting, for instance, Isaac was the one who started the petition to keep good books in the curriculum, even violent ones. He told John about it during their weekly phone call and received a barrage of kissing noises.

Over Christmas break, campus shut down for a couple days. Isaac reread John's novels in a desperate attempt to feel close to him. John might have hated his books—for now—but Isaac turned the pages with a lingering touch as though caressing John's skin. Everyone was busy, so Isaac spent the day alone. John's parents called to wish him a "Joyeux Noel," but he never heard from the man himself. A phone call days later confirmed that John had fought to ignore the holiday because he missed Isaac and his family too damn much.

To breach the gap, Isaac wrote John letters—disgusting, sweet things and sometimes boring things about the mundane everyday of Lothos. John never wrote back. On the phone, he said he was still learning to trust words again.

By the second month, Cleo started bringing huge casseroles to work and handing them to Isaac. "You look like Jack Skellington," she said. He wasn't eating much. Nothing tasted as good as John's cooking, and Isaac could barely drink coffee anymore because it never tasted *right*. More than once, he would think of a funny anecdote and look down and around, searching for John to tell him—but John wasn't there.

He and Tommy met several times a week for dinner or drinks. Some nights, they told "John stories;" other nights, when his absence was too heavy, they wouldn't even say his name. Isaac pretended to care about the close of college football season just to get Tommy to smile, but it didn't always work. Sometimes, they didn't speak at all—just sat together, drinking. John was the life vest on their sinking ship, so without him a sorrow oceans-wide lapped at their ankles and threatened to rise.

Being Frank functioned via stutters, starts, and sprints. As expected, the faculty—Meeks included—had been a bit put out by the students' decision to keep going with the literary magazine, but one look from Isaac and they'd all shut up. Meeks said he was acting like John, which was the biggest compliment she'd ever paid him.

However, he wasn't at all prepared for an invitation for drinks.

They met at some martini lounge—swanky and brightly lit off the Lothos main drag. Isaac wished he had sunglasses. He also sort of wanted full body armor, unsure of what the hell Meeks would have to say to him. He wasn't exactly her favorite person at the moment now that he was channeling John. She ordered a gin martini, and he ordered Knob Creek.

Maybe Isaac wasn't the only one losing sleep. He very much doubted Meeks had purposely put purple eye makeup *under* her eyes. With no preface at all, she said, "John won't be coming back to Hambden University."

Isaac's vision went white. He had to shake his head to regain blood flow. "What are you talking about?"

"He resigned." She slurped her cocktail.

"But—"

"To be with you."

His drink vibrated in his hand, so he put it down. "Oh, my God. What?"

"Based on the fact that he claims to be in love with you, I would have expected that you came to this decision together."

"No, I..." He scooted his drink away. He and John only had fifteen minutes of conversation once a week, but this did indeed seem like something they should have discussed. "He resigned?"

She ran a hand back over her hair. "Look, I don't know how long this thing has been going on between you. We are all well aware that interoffice romance breaks the code of conduct. Technically, I could have you fired." She sank lower in her seat. "But I wouldn't do that to the students." She tapped her finger on the base of her glass and looked anywhere but at him. "I'm proud of you, Isaac, and I do not say things like that lightly. You have become an unexpected strength on this campus, to your coworkers and to the kids. With John not coming back, it's going to be rough on them. They will need you to fill his space."

"No one can fill John's space."

"I know. I know, but we have to try. And keep going," Meeks said. "The school would like to offer you an extended contract, officially."

"I didn't even think you liked me."

She calmly sipped her drink. "I don't. Not really. But, for some reason, you fit here. You're one of us now. Plus, I think John would be very upset if he came back to find his boyfriend unemployed." She flipped her hair. "Men. You couldn't just keep it in your pants?"

He snorted, and Meeks cracked a smile.

"Make him happy," she said. "Or I'll ruin you."

They clinked glasses together and spent the next twenty minutes drinking in silence.

THANKFULLY, THE THIRD month without John was nonstop work insanity, which kept Isaac's mind off his missing lover, although he still went on the occasional night run that ended in tears on John's porch.

Isaac had made it through finals and the tedious reading of paper after boring paper. He'd also had the pleasure of standing in as guest instructor in John's creative writing courses, which flickered a creative flame in him he'd thought long extinguished. Maybe he'd even write again, too—someday. But the real chaos was thanks to *Being Frank*. Once the final favorite submissions had been chosen, editing began. Then, final cover art. Then, arranging the stories in proper thematic blocks. The list of "to do" went on and on, but Isaac's students seemed more driven than ever to see the project reach its final resounding conclusion.

Boxes back from the printers, they stood in a big circle, staring.

"We got to open it, man," Anthony said.

Isaac chewed his finger. "Just give me a minute."

"It won't bite."

"I wish John was here," Isaac said.

"We all do," said the mousy girl who'd stepped into Janelle's empty shoes.

Anthony poked his elbow into Isaac's ribs. "He'll be back in a week, right?"

A week. After all the time apart, and the final week might as well have been fifty years. Isaac often found himself watching clocks, counting the seconds. They'd talked on the phone only last night, John sounding chipper, but hesitant, almost like he was afraid of saying something offensive—or maybe afraid Isaac would finally give up and say, "I'm sorry, John, but I don't want to spend the rest of my life worrying about your mental health," when truly Isaac's mental health suffered without him.

"All right, let's see these things." Isaac tore off the blue mailing tape in one dramatic flourish.

Anthony reached his mitt into the box, hauling out the first-ever copy of *Being Frank*. He held it at arm's length and stared. "Shit, man, it looks good."

They'd gone with one of the more edgy photomontages, because punches were no longer being pulled around Hambden University. John's yell-first-think-later mentality had saturated the entire staff, filling the void of his absence with the power of his passion.

Isaac picked up his own copy. Abstract renderings of College Green shined glossy in shades of black and red, and in the very bottom corner, an eerie rendering of the faces of those lost, buried one on top of the other and including Chris Frank.

Isaac stumbled when Anthony gave him a bear hug. They both started laughing as other kids flipped through copies of *Being Frank*, differing emotions flying over faces: happiness, despair, excitement, and fear. So many emotions, but all good, because they were all honest.

ISAAC REVELED IN the hubbub of John's house, filled to the brim with people cleaning and decorating for his Sunday afternoon arrival. Adam—who'd shamelessly pinched Isaac's butt when he walked in—scrubbed the bathroom, while Sasha worked in the kitchen. Cleo obsessively rearranged a tray of beignets, trying so hard to be artfully French. Isaac found Tommy hanging an Ohio State flag in the living room and said, "You wouldn't dare," in his most dramatic Broadway voice.

Tommy grinned. "What?"

"I'll burn it."

"Man, he has you whipped." Tommy folded the flag and tossed it on the couch. "I'm guessing you don't want us here on Sunday so that you can ravish him like a Victorian maiden?"

"Uh, well." Isaac nodded. "Yeah. Yeah, pretty much."

Adam swept by—"I called this shit in October"—before grabbing Windex and disappearing back down the hall.

Cleo snapped her manicured fingers. "The kitchen should be fully stocked with all John's favorite food and ingredients for cooking his most famous dishes. Plus, coffee, lots of coffee."

But no alcohol. John had decided to give up drinking for the foreseeable future.

"Are the linens clean in the bedroom?"

Isaac patted her shoulder. "I'll take care of it, Cleo."

"Dr. Twain, everything needs to be perfect!" She flapped her hands before wandering away, talking to herself: "Flowers; I need to buy flowers." Her rose perfume imitated her shopping list.

He and Tommy remained.

"He's going to be okay this time," Tommy said. "I can feel it."

"You don't have to convince me."

"No. I just wanted to say it." He took off his glasses and wiped them on his wrinkled shirt. "The house feels weird without him, huh?"

Isaac chuckled. "You have no idea."

"The patter of his little feet."

"He doesn't have little feet."

Tommy smiled. "No, you're right. They look like clown shoes." He took a step closer and looked both ways. "Don't take this the wrong way, but I sort of love you, man."

"I get it," Isaac said.

They nodded in sync.

"Well, I have to go." Tommy reached for his coat on the back of a chair. "Hot date."

"Purple-headed Halloween chick?"

"Isaac, she has a name. You've met her, like, fifteen times."

Isaac leaned back on his heels. "I like her nickname more."

Cue familiar John eye roll on Tommy's face.

Cleo stayed later than everyone else. She and Isaac sat in the living room, drinking tea, discussing the new semester. They tried very hard not to talk about John's noticeable absence in Ellis Hall. The lack of his presence was like a ghost everybody could see but nobody talked about. It would get better. It had to.

She left just as the sun sank over John's backyard, blanketed in glittering, white snow. Isaac watched the stillness of the trees for a while before prepping for some random TV and bed. Big day tomorrow: the official launch of *Being Frank*. Before falling asleep, he prayed everything would go well.

THEY HAD A table in the student union, right near the entrance, so yes, it was freezing—but no one could get in without seeing the gigantic banner that read, *"Being Frank: Healing through the Written Word."* Meeks had already been by to get her copy, and she had yet to run back in, screaming, so she must have approved of the final product. Anthony had video chatted with Janelle. Despite her exit speech, Janelle did keep in touch with her old friend—and Anthony said she even smiled sometimes.

Isaac's sales technique was eye contact. If he could catch a student's eye, maybe smile, they usually came over to the table. Others rushed past, not even looking, but he couldn't fault them for their reaction. Healing took strength and time.

Around lunch, things picked up. They were basically mauled for copies and battered by questions. Kids wanted to know why they'd done it. Why focus an entire magazine on something so awful? Anthony usually spoke up first. He liked to tell people, "It's about being real. It happened. It was real." Isaac had a feeling his loud-mouthed star pupil might rule the world one day.

Isaac was trying to keep the table in some kind of order. As opposed to having magazines strewn all over the place, he fought to keep them in stacks, although it was a battle lost to grabby hands and enthusiasm.

He was arranging just such a stack when a voice asked, "Can I get a copy?"

His fingers froze as he looked up to find John standing there. John, pale as ever with those green eyes and cheekbones and slightly slumped shoulders. *His John.*

Isaac almost flipped the table in his rush to get to John and lift him up into a kiss. John responded instantly, wrapping his arms around Isaac's shoulders as Isaac lifted his feet from the floor and kissed and rubbed his nose across John's cheek and kissed some more.

Anthony hooted. "Holy shit, you're gay for each other? I need a picture."

John laughed into Isaac's mouth, but Isaac wasn't done kissing. He kissed until he remembered that John's mouth felt like a sun-warmed peach and that he smelled like witch hazel and that he felt small and perfect in his arms.

He eventually pulled back but kept their noses touching. "You're early."

"I wanted to surprise you. And I didn't want to miss this." He gestured with his hand toward the banner—and all the students who now stared at them, grinning.

Anthony was the first to move. "Out of my way. Dr. Twain, man, give a guy a turn."

With great reluctance, Isaac set John's feet on the ground, and half the students mobbed him, wrapping him in hugs that shook back and forth with excitement or shuddered, ever so gently, with tears. Isaac caught Anthony wiping his eyes before the youngster exclaimed, "Hey, I'm cool. I'm cool. Look away."

Witnessing their scene, students entering the student union stopped and reached for copies of the magazine.

Following a final kiss to John's forehead, Isaac—and the *Being Frank* staff—resumed position behind the table.

John picked up a copy and started to read. He flipped a few pages, and Isaac knew when he saw the dedication page, knew the words he read. Although Anthony had suggested they include Janelle and John on that page of acknowledgment, the staff had gone with something more inclusive: *To those lost on College Green. And to the ones who lived.*

John wiped his face on his shoulder. "You assholes." He sniffed. "I told myself I wasn't going to cry today."

Chapter Nineteen

SINCE NOVEMBER, ISAAC had pretty much been living at John's house, but with John back, they decided to make it official. Isaac threw his measly clothes collection on John's bed and opened the closet—which was fit to bursting.

"Why do you own so many clothes?" he shouted down the hall, noting at least three different pairs of Converse sneakers. He heard the *tap-tap* of John's bare feet coming closer and pulled out a frankly alarming shirt with red hearts all over it. "I have never seen you wear this."

John plucked it from his hand. "What are you talking about? I just wore that three years ago."

"It's gay, even for you." Isaac laughed.

"Hey," John sang and melted back onto the bed, legs hanging over the edge. "Maybe I'll have to get rid of some stuff. I've never lived with anyone before, remember?"

It had been at least five minutes since they'd kissed, so Isaac jumped on the bed, almost propelling John right off. They grabbed onto each other just in time. "Yes. I remember." He kissed him—and kissed him some more.

They had spent the entire weekend having sex, eating French pastries, and drinking coffee—because John was back and no one made coffee like John. No one made love like John either. Isaac didn't even shower after. They'd had a long talk about that, but in the end...

"Do you feel bad about having sex with me?"

"No."

"Does it feel like a sin?"

"No."

"Do you think God is angry with you for loving me?"

"I think God brought you into my life."

They had then kissed for an hour.

Sunday afternoon, Isaac gave John space to write. There would be off days—days when he didn't trust himself, when the words were gremlins tearing his skin—but he was creating, and his therapist believed John was happiest when creating. That was part of why he'd resigned from Hambden; he wanted to write full-time. His agent was supportive, as was his publisher, but Isaac was ecstatic. Another John Conlon book? He would have given his big toe.

THEIR SWEATY CHESTS separated with a slurping suction cup sound as Isaac leaned up on his elbows above John, face turned to the side, mouth wide open. Isaac swept a couple curls behind his ear. "Wow, you look fucked out."

"Mmph," John muttered and wrinkled his nose.

Isaac sucked the side of John's neck. "Seriously, you look like someone who just took a ride in a washing machine."

"Well, I definitely took a ride." He dug the side of his face farther into the pillow and sighed out two big breaths like he'd been saving them.

"Be right back." Isaac rolled off his lover and did an awkward walk to the bathroom where he tossed the used condom in the trash and washed his hands. While drying off, he stared at the two toothbrushes on the counter. A slight tremor ran up the backs of his legs that had him clawing at the wall for balance.

Isaac had experienced a couple of those moments—moments of panic over reminders that John was back but that he had also been gone. Two toothbrushes instead of one indicated in some dark corner of Isaac's brain that it could be just one again. He could be alone in John's house again.

Naked, he rushed back to the bedroom but stopped in the doorway. John was still there, half lit by the antique table lamp, not a ghostly manifestation but the man himself. On his side with his knees curled up, John rested with his mouth open, still panting out hurried breaths as he recovered from their lovemaking. John was there and safe, so Isaac took steps forward and reached for him. He dove under the expensive sheets and took hold of John with one hand on his shoulder, the other on his hip. The sudden movement startled John, big eyes open, suddenly awake and staring at Isaac.

"Hmm." John's fingertips rubbed over Isaac's lips.

"Have I mentioned I missed you?"

John gifted a sleepy smile. "Every day since I've been back."

Isaac nibbled his fingers before pressing a kiss to each one. "Promise you'll never go away again."

John's legs straightened, and his eyes, drowsy a moment ago, burned with an almost manic alertness. "I can't promise you that."

Isaac's breath trembled on an inhale as he pulled John close with his hand on the back of his head. He pressed kiss after kiss to his forehead and to his eyelids, and John let him, the tension mostly gone but lingering below the surface like contained electric current.

A few hours later, something woke Isaac: a sound, a whimper. He reached for John's hand but found nothing but tense muscle, so he turned on the light. John was rolled into a small ball, hands covering his head. Isaac tried to touch him, and he screamed.

"John." He reached for him again, and John pulled his knees in tighter.

He mumbled, "No, no, no..." Soaked tendrils of hair covered his cheeks like claws.

"John. Please."

He shouted and hit himself in the head.

Isaac caught his flailing wrist. "John!"

John shuddered and sat up, gasping for breath like a man half drowned. His wide eyes took in his surroundings and landed on Isaac before he bent forward, sobbing. Isaac pulled him into his arms and held tight enough to leave marks.

"I've got you," he said.

John huffed and puffed, sucking air. His entire body quivered from fear and from the cold sweat that covered his skin.

"Stay with me, John."

"You were dead," he whispered. "You were dead."

"I'm not dead. And neither are you."

Eventually, they lay down again, arms and legs tangled beneath sheets. John fell asleep quickly, face against Isaac's bare chest. Isaac stayed awake, focused on the sound of John's breath.

"What dreams may come," Isaac mumbled, and they would come, wouldn't they? No matter how many demons they had faced, there would always be more. Memories would linger in the dark corners of their minds as healing turned to happiness. But even happiness hid its face some days. One step at a time, they would walk together, even as the dead walked among them, too—even when the dead sometimes clung to their shoulders—because, no matter their losses, they still lived.

About the Author

Sara Dobie Bauer is a bestselling author, model, and mental health / LGBTQ advocate with a creative writing degree from Ohio University. She lives with her hottie husband and two precious pups in Northeast Ohio, although she'd really like to live in a Tim Burton film. She is author of the paranormal rom-com Bite Somebody series and Escape Trilogy.

Email: sara@saradobie.com

Facebook: www.facebook.com/AuthorSaraDobieBauer

Sara Dobie Bauer's Sexy Circle:
www.facebook.com/groups/SaraDobieBauer

Twitter: @SaraDobie

Website: www.saradobiebauer.com

Freebies and newsletter sign up:
www.saradobiebauer.com/freebies

Other books by this author

Escaping Exile
Escaping Solitude
Escaping Mortality

Also Available from NineStar Press

Connect with NineStar Press

www.ninestarpress.com

www.facebook.com/ninestarpress

www.facebook.com/groups/NineStarNiche

www.twitter.com/ninestarpress

www.tumblr.com/blog/ninestarpress